Monster STEPBROTHER

HIS DARK OBSESSION RUNS DEEP

International Bestselling Author
Harlow Grace

WARNING:
Not appropriate for readers under 18.
Contains dark and sensitive subject matter that may make readers uncomfortable.
Contains explicit language and descriptions of sexual situations.

Please respect the work of this author and do not violate copyright laws.

No part of this book may be distributed for commercial or non-commercial purposes, copied, or reproduced electronically or in print without written permission, except for brief quotations embodied for reviews.

This book is licensed for your personal enjoyment only.

Thank you for respecting the hard work —hours upon hours of blood, sweat and tears and sleepless nights—of this author poured into this novel.

This is a work of fiction. Names, characters, places, and incidents are products of the author's imagination or are used fictitiously and are not to be construed as real.

Any resemblance to actual events, locales, organizations, or persons, living or dead, is entirely coincidental.

Editor
Dawn Daniels (Daniels.dawn14@gmail.com)

Cover Designer
Mayhem Cover Creations

Formatting
Interface Publishing (interfacepublishing@gmail.com)

Copyright © 2015 Harlow Grace
All rights reserved.

ISBN: 978-1508816546

DEDICATION

To my beautiful daughter.
You are the reason I strive to be a better person every day.

To my partner in crime.
You inspire me. I got lucky when you came into my life.

Prologue
OLIVER

AND SO IT BEGAN: **Six years ago**

Spotting the familiar face in the crowd, I moved in the direction of the threesome waiting for me at the airport. My flight had been delayed by an hour and that made me cranky, as did most things these days.

I couldn't help noticing how wide my mother's smile had grown. She looked so damn content standing there with her new family that I didn't really know why she'd insisted that I leave my friends to come to this place during the summer vacation. I shoved my way through the throngs of people blocking my path as they reunited with those waiting for them, grimacing as my gaze fell on my new stepsister. I'd only seen her once before, at the wedding, and that was more than enough for me.

The kid looked up at me with huge green eyes and a sweet smile. It irritated the shit out of me. I already hated her and her father for making my mother move back there from Los Angeles. "Hi, Oliver," she said as I approached, dimples appearing in each cheek. "Welcome back."

I grunted something back at her, pissed off because she was being sweet to me. If anyone thought I was going to play the role of an adoring older brother, I had a surprise waiting for them—all I wanted was for her to stay the fuck out of my way.

I glared at my new stepfather. He was standing behind the gangly kid, his hand resting on her shoulder and squeezing lightly. *He* was to blame for all this bullshit.

My gaze shifted to my mother who stood beside the distinguished-looking man with graying temples and a welcoming smile. Hooked into his arm, she leaned forward to kiss my cheek. "Oliver, I'm so happy that you've come. Sorry your flight was delayed, honey; I know how you hate that."

"Hey, Mom," I said, not even cracking a smile.

She kept up the overly friendly chatter like she always did when she was nervous. "Once we get home, you can relax and take a swim. I cooked your favorite meal for dinner. Maya has already set the table—she's that excited to see her stepbrother."

Maya stood there grinning up at me as if she was waiting for me to pet her head like a puppy. "I picked flowers from the garden for your bedroom. I'm so glad you're going to stay for a few weeks this time. Maybe we can hang out?" she said, all bright and bubbly.

My stomach churned. *Jesus, this love fest is going to make me sick.* I didn't want any part of it.

Once I was legally an adult, I wasn't returning if I could help it. Until then, I'd have to grin and bear it—my inheritance didn't kick in until my eighteenth birthday. It was going to be the longest two years of my screwed-up life.

"Hello, Oliver," my stepdad said, crinkles forming at the corners of his eyes. I looked away, ignoring the older man's outstretched hand as I pulled my mother into a quick hug, then let her go and headed for the carousel to collect my luggage.

Fifteen minutes later, I was staring out the car window as we drove to my mother's new home. The kid sat silently beside me, her gaze drinking me in. I was glad everyone had stopped their happy chattering from earlier; it made my head hurt.

"What are you staring at?" I snarled, unnerved by the way she made me feel—as if her eyes saw right through me. She was twelve going on twenty.

Lowering her head, she bit into her lip and studied her nails. She had beautiful hands with long sleek fingers. Her brows knitted together and her mouth turned downward. She was hurt, but what the fuck did I care? I'd be gone before long.

Both my mother and her new husband tried to engage me in conversation on the ride back to their place, but they quickly gave up when I just grunted a "yes" or "no" in response. Mom sighed and placed her palm on the prick's lap. He squeezed her hand and then turned his head to smile at her.

"Hey, old man, eyes on the road." Ever since my dad had died in a car accident not far from there, I couldn't stand when people didn't give driving their full attention.

"It's okay, sweetheart—Alec is a good driver. He's much more careful than your father. He'll get us home safely."

That comment made my blood boil. "Why would you say shit like that about my father?"

"Sorry. I didn't mean it like that," she said as she squirmed in her seat.

"We need to have a talk when we get to the house," the old man threatened.

"Like hell. Just because you're married to my mother, that doesn't make you my father." I turned to the kid, whose head had snapped up. Her eyes widened in shock. "Nor does that make this kid my sister. So don't expect me to be nice or brotherly or any of that screwed up shit. I'm not going to play happy families with you."

Mom sucked in a breath, but didn't say anything. She knew how I felt about her coming back to the place that had caused us so much unhappiness. Why couldn't she have met and married someone in LA and started her new life there instead of running back to this place and dumping me at boarding school?

Apparently big cities weren't for her and she missed Santa Barbara. *Yeah right.* I doubted that was true after everything we'd been through in the years we'd lived there. A few weeks later the truth came out. She was marrying a plastic surgeon—she'd known the guy even before my dad's accident. He'd been making a killing off her cosmetic surgery addiction. Hell, she'd probably paid for this car with the amount of work she'd had done.

My stepfather patted Mom's hand reassuringly. "Larissa, sweetheart, don't be upset. Oliver and I will have a man-to-man talk about his attitude when we get to the house."

Groaning, I folded my arms across my chest. Great. Now my attitude was a problem. What the fuck did he expect? For me to be all sweet with everything that happened in spite of being left to fend for myself in LA?

I caught a glimpse of the kid's face. *Pity.* That's what she was feeling for me. I didn't need a kid four years younger feeling sorry for me. That was just fucked up.

Pissed off, I turned my body away and watched the scenery as we drove by, hating everything I saw. To no one in particular, I said, "Yeah, judge me. How would you feel if your mother married someone only six months after your father died, and you were forced to go back to a place you hated?"

Yeah, I had issues. Anger management being only one of them.

Nobody said a word. *Good.* Silence was far better. The kid turned to stare out of the window and Alec squeezed Mom's hand. I plugged my earphones in and turned up the music until it drowned everything else out.

I had a plan—I'd stay in my bedroom for most of the time, maybe swim during the day, but otherwise I was avoiding everyone until it was time to go back to LA.

And the kid? If she knew what was good for her, she'd stay the fuck out of my way. I certainly didn't need her sweet ways or her pity. What would she know about being abandoned by a parent? She didn't have a fucking clue..

Chapter 1
MAYA

PRESENT

"Maya! What the fuck? What the hell have you done?" Oliver's voice droned through the emptiness to my foggy brain. I couldn't be sure if the panic in his voice was real or imagined. It was difficult to decipher his words. Rage was all I heard. All I felt.

It was nothing new. Fury burned inside him—and me. Since the beginning, anger and contempt steadily intensified until it became all-consuming. Destructive.

Pain shot through my arm. Alarmed, I let the blade drop from my fingers.

Red. So much red.

It covered my skin and the floor I sat on. I never knew I had this much blood in my body. It was everywhere. I slumped forward and closed my eyes. Oliver reached out and gripped my chin, jerking my face towards his while he painfully squeezed my cheeks together. Fighting the heaviness of my eyelids, I managed to pry them open enough to see his angst-ridden face inches from mine. I slowly exhaled, consciousness threatening to leave me.

"Answer me, goddammit. What's going on?"

Can't you see?

My leaden limbs sunk deeper into the floor until numbness took over. My eyes tried to focus on his, but it was too difficult. I couldn't keep them open any longer. Heavy, they fluttered closed and surrendered to darkness.

"Fuck. You're not dying on me. Breathe, Maya. Fucking *breathe*." His voice boomed through the silence, echoing off the tile. Hollow—the same as what my life had become. If I weren't in so much agony, I'd laugh.

Shivering as my body slid to the cold floor, I couldn't stop my teeth from clattering. Fear gripped my insides, turning my stomach into a whirlpool as I sank deeper into the darkness.

"Stay awake. Maya, stay the fuck awake. Open your fucking eyes."

Yeah, like I want to listen to you.

My stepbrother had been nothing but mean to me since the first day he came to this house. And even now, in these last minutes, he was still trying to tell me what to do.

No fucking way. I've had enough.

My teeth rattled as the grip on my arms tightened—my stepbrother was shaking me vigorously. "Leave me the fuck alone," I managed to squeeze out, wishing the Reaper would hurry up and get me out of here. It was the last cruel joke I'd have to endure—that of all the people in the world, it was Oliver King who found me, covered in my own blood, on my way to heaven.

Or hell.

Either way, I don't give a shit where I go, as long as it isn't here.

Full, warm lips touched mine, forcing unwanted air into my lungs. *His air.* I tried to press my lips together, tried to stop the oxygen from reaching my lungs.

I don't want his fucking breath inside of me.

Why was he doing this to me? Why couldn't he just let my miserable life end in fucking peace? But no, the bastard always had to have the last say. Even now.

Before Summertime in Santa Barbara

Chapter 2
OLIVER

TWO YEARS AGO

In spite of my best intentions to avoid visiting my mother and her new family, it was Larissa's fortieth birthday in a week and she'd begged me to come "home." Since I'd missed her last birthday, I'd decided to surprise her, taking a taxi from the airport to the mansion she shared with her new husband and the kid.

Maybe I wouldn't hate the place as much now that I'd been away for nearly two years. It was college midterm break anyway, and I needed to relax, so I figured lazing around the pool in the Californian sun wasn't such a bad idea. At least the old man had good taste in all things material—the three story house was impeccable and was surrounded by perfectly landscaped gardens, with a gigantic pool and plants that reminded me of the tropical paradises I'd seen pictures of in travel brochures. Set against the hill, the spectacular ocean views never failed to take my breath away.

Besides, I was tired of eating rubbish and was in need of a decent cooked meal. My mother wasn't particularly good at most things not involving her looks, but she was a great hostess and a good cook and I missed her food.

After paying the taxi fare, I grabbed my bags and made my way through the fancy iron gates. The house had been freshly painted and rows of pink roses lined the pathway. The rose bushes definitely weren't there the last time I came to Santa Barbara for my eighteenth birthday, so I knew my mother must've had them planted. She loved flowers, especially roses.

Once my inheritance had paid out I'd left as quickly as I could, promising myself that I wouldn't come back unless I absolutely had to. This was one such occasion I couldn't avoid without upsetting my mother.

I rang the doorbell, my heartbeat quickening as I waited for someone to answer. I shuffled from one foot to the other for a full three minutes before pushing the button again. The chime of the doorbell echoed through the house, but I couldn't hear any footsteps.

Fuck. *That's what happens when you decide to surprise someone.* I'd have to get my own key so that I wouldn't be left standing at the front door again. The bunch of flowers in my arm withered in the heat, and I was in need of a long, cool drink.

I decided to go around to the pool where I planned to spend most of my time anyway. Alec kept a well-stocked bar on the patio and there was certain to be a beer with my name on it in the bar fridge. Images of the frosty beverage sliding down my throat made me smile and walk just a little faster in spite of the heat draining me. Maybe it wasn't such a bad thing after all that nobody was home. I could settle in and just chill out for a while before being bombarded with Mom's thousand and one questions. Or having to face the *step*family.

I'd have a swim and relax for a bit, enjoying the scenery and listening to music on my iPod while waiting for Mom to return. I strolled toward the deck and placed my shit on a chair. The flowers appeared to be beyond saving, but I found a pitcher and placed them in water anyway.

Grinning, I opened the fridge and found a bottle of imported beer. I gulped it down, hardly tasting the amber liquid. Letting out a satisfying burp, I wiped my mouth with the back of my hand, ready for a swim.

The pool area was green and lush, with sprinklers dancing across the rolling lawns. Eager to cool off, I stripped to my boxers, ready to dive straight into the water. I walked lazily toward the pool, not a care in the world. I'd get a start on my tan, and still surprise Mom when she got home.

My head jerked up when I heard water splashing. Who was in the pool? Squinting my eyes against the sun, I made out a dark head. *The kid.* Fuck. Not her. Grimacing, my stomach dropped—I was looking forward to peace and quiet and being by myself for a while, and I wasn't ready for her yet.

Maya swam another lap underwater before her head bobbed up for a few moments to take in air. Then she disappeared again, swimming toward the steps. I stopped dead in my tracks as she lifted herself out of the water and shook her head, her long, dark hair fanning out as water dripped off it, her face tilted up to the sky.

My gaze lowered to her chest. Shit. She had grown a pair of tits. Perky tits with hard nipples that pushed against the fabric of her bikini top. Her golden skin was covered with goose bumps. My cock twitched.

What the fuck?

No. Just fucking *no.*

Not the fucking kid.

No way in hell did I want her to affect me like that. Not that it stopped me from gawking. Taking in her long legs, flat stomach, and hips that should be illegal on a sixteen year old, I cursed under my breath. The kid was beautiful. Breathtaking.

Yet of all her features, it was her naturally reddish bee-sting lips that intrigued me most. With a fuller lower lip and perfectly formed cupid's bow, they just about filled her face.

Her head jerked toward me, her mouth falling open when she noticed me. "Jesus, you scared me," she scolded, a frown drawing her eyebrows together. "What the hell are you doing here?"

No smile. No words of welcome.

"You have a dirty mouth for a kid," I said, my eyes still on her body, drinking it all in. The white bikini bottom had crawled up her ass and pulled tightly around her pussy, making her mound stand proud, ripe, and ready for picking. It was impossible not to notice the changes or get a hard-on. I could strip her naked and bang the shit out of her in an instant.

She rolled her eyes at me, reminding me that although she'd grown up a hell of a lot since I'd last seen her, she was still just a moody teenager. *Beautiful* moody teenager with a gorgeous body I couldn't tear my eyes away from. Thank fuck I hadn't stripped down my boxers, or else my erection would be throbbing between us with nothing to hide it. The last thing I wanted was for her to know how much she was having an effect on me.

Her eyes flashed with irritation. "I'm not a kid any more, as if you haven't noticed. My eyes are up here, asshole." She lifted her chin in defiance.

"Yeah, I noticed all right," I drawled, still getting my head around how much she had changed and how that was making me crazy. What the fuck was wrong with me?

Like it or not, the kid was family. Stepfamily, but still *family*. I wasn't going there. At least that was what I kept telling myself. My stomach turned when I remembered how her sweet smile and soulful eyes had distressed me when I first saw her all those years ago. As a sixteen-year-old I hadn't had any idea how to process it. All I knew was that it was wrong on so many levels, and so I'd pushed those awkward feelings way the fuck down, turning the darkness in me up a notch to hide what I daren't let anyone suspect.

I'd made up my mind that I wasn't going to like her, and back then I managed it pretty well. However, what I was experiencing at that moment wasn't working with my master plan. If I kept hatred or at least indifference between us, I'd be okay. But my dick had other plans. Plans I didn't like one bit. I wasn't out of the woods. Far from it. In fact, the hazard had just escalated to being in the danger zone.

I hated not being in control. It freaked me the fuck out.

And Maya made me lose all sense of control.

"So what made you decide to honor us with your presence?" She crossed her arms over her chest in an attempt to hide her tits from me, but it only made it worse—she was actually pushing them up.

Tearing my eyes away from her cleavage, my gaze drifted back to her green eyes. Specks of gold glistened in the sunlight. My mouth dry, I said, "Larissa's birthday. It's important to her."

"Well, stay out of my way," she said before smacking her palms hard against my chest to shove me away.

Grinding my teeth together, I grabbed hold of her wrists and held them in an iron grip. I didn't like little bitches taunting me. Her gaze snapped to mine, fire lighting her eyes as she held her own. Her full lips were inches from mine, wet and dewy. Shit. Besides growing a spectacular pair of tits, she'd grown some balls too. The shy, gangly kid with the friendly smile had evaporated and been replaced with a killer body and a fuck-off attitude.

"Let me go, Oliver," she said, her nostrils flaring. Her warm breath puffed against my chest and sent a chill up my spine.

Her obstinance turned me on even more, to the point that I was hardly able to think straight. "What's wrong, little bee?"

"Little bee?" She tilted her head and watched my face, smirking.

"Yeah. Ever watch Maya *the Bee?*"

"Um . . . only since I started watching TV as a toddler. It's old, Oliver. Everyone called me Maya the Bee or something like that in preschool and elementary school."

I sneered. "Well, *little bee,* I figure you have a serious sting in that tail. I'm allergic to bees, though."

"Tell someone who cares," she said with venom in her voice.

"You have way too much of a smart mouth, *kid.*"

I hated how she'd grown up. Hated how she'd smart-mouthed me. *How she affected me.* How I was powerless to control it. My body trembled as I fought to stop the urge to shake her. Instead I dropped her hands, took a step to the side, and dived into the cold water to calm my dick—and mind—the fuck down.

My little stepsister was jail bait. I had no intention of getting stung.

Chapter 3
OLIVER

Maya disappeared into the house and didn't show her face again until dinner time. Just as well; I didn't need any more of her snarky attitude. Or the disturbing way she made me feel.

Scowling, I remembered how I was at her age. Always infuriated, I was a ticking time-bomb. Since then I'd mellowed enough to control my feelings most of the time. Although I still carried that anger inside me, I'd gotten better at hiding it. She'd learn just as I had. It was a matter of time until she outgrew the awkward teenage stage. And anyone with eyes in their heads could tell Maya was going to be a stunner as a woman. As much as I hated admitting it, my cock had certainly picked up on that.

Making up my mind to avoid her as much as possible during my stay, I decided to work on my tan and get into some hardcore exercise at the home gym. Alec had a whole room decked out with the latest fitness equipment and I planned to put it to good use in the next three weeks. I was proud of my body and worked hard to keep fit. It helped with my studies too; concentrating and working on computers all day to get a degree in IT meant I didn't have much time for anything else, but I always made it a priority to keep my body in top shape.

Mom had returned from her hairdressing appointment half an hour ago, and we spent a while on the veranda catching up with one another's news. I'd succeeded in surprising her, so that was a positive. She invited me inside and started cooking. I poured her a glass of wine and grabbed a beer from the fridge, then made myself comfortable on a high stool and watched as she chopped the vegetables, filling her in on the highlights of the past two years of college.

Although the flowers I'd brought had wilted, she placed them in a crystal vase on the expansive granite kitchen counter near the window.

"You look pretty settled in here. I noticed you planted roses out front."

I hadn't quite been a model son, but I really wanted her to be happier than she'd been with my father. Sipping on my drink, I listened to her, nodding occasionally as she told me about her new life.

"I'm so happy, Oliver. Moving back here was one of the best things I've ever done. I know it sucks for you to stay alone in LA, but at least you have your uncle Barry close by to help you out." She paused and took a deep breath. "If only—"

"*Yeah?*" I took another sip of beer and waited for her to continue.

"Maya and I don't quite gel," she said matter-of-factly. "So we kinda stay out of one another's way as much as possible."

Larissa was a beautiful woman and I knew she didn't like competition—even from her best friends. I couldn't blame her for feeling a bit threatened by the kid.

"Did I hear my name?" Maya sauntered into the kitchen. She wore a pair of shorts that hugged her ass and a loose top that dropped off one shoulder in a casual manner. She wasn't wearing a bra; as she leaned down to get a plate from the cupboard, I could look down her top. Her tits were just enough for a handful. The perfect size for my palm.

Fuck. Why am I thinking about her like that?

Ignoring her question, Mom lifted a brow, scowling as she took in the slutty appearance of her stepdaughter. "It would be nice if you dressed more appropriately while Oliver is visiting."

Maya turned to her and smiled sweetly, but it didn't reach her eyes. "Scared I'll seduce my stepbrother, Mommy Dearest?" Her gaze swung to me. She pulled up her pretty little nose. "He's not my type, actually. I'm a little pickier than that."

Yep, there's that sting again.

Next she was back in front of the open fridge, bending over to take a few carrots and some fruit from the cold-drawer. Her shorts pulled further up her perfect ass, displaying her smooth-as-silk skin.

"I won't be down for dinner tonight. I'm on a diet." She walked away without waiting for my mother's response.

Mom's face flushed with anger. "Suit your damn self," she mumbled before emptying her wine glass and holding it out to me for a refill. "God, I wouldn't wish a sixteen-year-old stepdaughter on my worst enemy."

Strangely glad I wasn't the only one who was aggravated by my stepsister, I laughed. "I'm going down to the club after dinner. A few of my college friends live in Santa Barbara, and they said to join them tonight. They're picking me up at nine."

I filled her glass and handed it back to her. She immediately took another swig before placing it down and resumed chopping carrots—only this time she slammed the knife hard and fast.

"That's great that you're going out with friends. The only night I need you home is for my party on Saturday, of course."

I leaned in and kissed her on her cheek. "I wouldn't miss that occasion for anything. And for what it's worth, you look great, so you have nothing to worry about."

She straightened her hair and smiled up at me. "I needed to hear that. Thanks." She smoothed her hands over her hips. "It's not easy getting older."

I gave her a reassuring hug.

"I'm going upstairs to unpack my bag and have a shower. When should I come down for dinner?"

"In an hour. Alec and I like to relax over a glass of wine when he gets home, so come join us, okay?"

Grimacing, I nodded. I'd have to face the old man sooner or later. But right now I needed a shower to wash off the chlorine from the pool and get ready for a night out. Brent had called me earlier to tell me that Bianca, the busty Scandinavian blonde who took one of the same classes I did, was coming to stay with her uncle for the vacation. I grinned at the thought. Yeah, I remembered Bianca. I'd banged her senseless after the last frat party I'd been to in LA and looked forward to more of her in my near future. She'd help to keep my balls empty and my mind off a certain sixteen year old. Perfect.

Whistling as I went up the stairs, I inwardly high-fived myself. I'd have dinner and laundry sorted for the next three weeks, work on my tan during the day, and screw Bianca until she couldn't walk. Life was looking good.

As I passed Maya's bedroom, I saw her spread out on her bed. She was talking softly to someone on her phone. A boy? I stopped for a second just outside her door, my gaze drinking in the long legs that were propped up against the wall. Her hair hung over the edge of the bed, so long that it nearly touched the floor.

Mesmerized, my gaze was glued to her athletic body. I watched as her hand stroked slowly over her ribs and bared stomach, then held my breath as it disappeared under her shorts. *Definitely a fucking boy.* I froze for a long moment as I listened to her voice. The tone was soft, sexy even. My stomach twisted into a knot and heat rose to my neck. She was too young to be talking sexy to boys.

As if she sensed my presence, she turned her head, her eyes narrowing as she saw me. She didn't acknowledge me; instead she turned her face away and pulled her hand from her shorts. Good. I let out a long breath, relieved that she wasn't going there.

It was short lived. My eyes widened as her hand pushed under her top and cupped her boob. I couldn't see everything through the fabric half covering her tits, but she squeezed her breast and moaned softly before twisting her nipple between her fingers.

Jesus Christ! I reached out to hold on to the doorjamb, licking my lips as I kept on watching. Little vixen was just warming up. She pinched the phone between her chin and shoulder and used both hands to undo the buttons of her shorts. Shit. I wasn't going anywhere, and she knew it. Heat spread like wildfire around my groin, and my jeans expanded to stretch over my hard-on.

She licked the tips of her fingers before lowering her hand back down under her shorts. As she spread her legs wider, I could see that her pussy was smooth. The aroma of her arousal drifted to my nostrils, driving me to the edge of insanity. I could virtually taste her on my tongue.

My cock strained harder against the damp boxers and jeans I had slipped back on, fighting to be set free and sink into her pussy. My throat tightened. Fuck. I could feel my heartbeat in my cock.

Maya moaned softly as her fingers moved back and forth while her free hand ran over her ribs, pushing up her top to expose one breast. The nipple, pink as a rosebud, stood erect. She pulled on her nipple, her head falling further back over the edge of the bed so I could see her face. Her eyes were squeezed shut. Her cheeks flushed pink, a glow misting over her skin as she bit hard into her lower lip.

My hand rested on my concrete cock, eager to partake in the scene unfolding before me. It wanted in—desperately.

Her teeth set her lip free and she whimpered as her body shuddered. Her eyes flew open and sought mine, locking on to my unwavering stare. A smile twisted the corners of her mouth as she let out a long low moan. I could easily come in my pants; it was that hot.

Her smile widened as she brought her fingers to her mouth and sucked her juices off them one by one. Fucking little tease. The whole room smelled like her—there was no way in hell I was getting that scent out of my head any time soon.

Maya told the boy to hang on, removing the phone from her ear.

"Was that good for you, too?" she said, her eyes boring into mine, smiling as if butter couldn't melt in her mouth.

Chapter 4
OLIVER

After the party I brought Bianca back to the house. She was definitely tipsy and ready to be fucked hard. I'd already stripped her panties off and gone down on her thirty minutes after arriving at the party. I'd pushed her into the bathroom and sucked and licked her pussy, eating her out like a madman, all the time imagining tasting another pussy on my tongue.

Signaling for her to be quiet, we tiptoed up the stairs. Maya's bedroom door was closed, but I could see light streaming from under it. *Good, she's still awake.* Bianca stumbled into my room and fell onto the bed, giggling as she pulled up her dress to expose herself to me. My balls were ready to explode from the afternoon's episode, so I didn't want to waste any time getting my dick wet. Thirty seconds later, my jeans hit the floor and my cock sprang free.

Rolling on a condom, I pushed Bianca's legs apart and crawled over her. I was going in hard. "Open wide, babe," I grunted as I pushed into her.

"Jesus!" she cried out as I rammed my cock into her. Groping her tits, I squeezed hard, imagining what sixteen-year-old breasts felt like. I felt dirty but oh-so fucking turned on. I gripped hold of Bianca's hair and pulled her head back as I slammed my cock into her, trying my best to obliterate the vision of a dark-haired girl that flashed through my mind. The headboard thumped against the wall with every thrust, rattling the pictures in stereo until I let out a roar and came so hard I nearly passed out.

The face was still there—along with the image of her tits and her hand down her shorts. I cursed out loud and slapped Bianca's ass, hard, smiling as she cried out my name. Although I'd had release, I didn't feel any better. My dick was still hard as hell knowing Maya was just on the other side of a thin wall and had probably heard everything.

"Turn around," I ordered as I pulled my cock from Bianca's pussy and flipped her over. "Hold on to the headboard and don't let go. This is going to get rough."

"Oliver," she screamed as I speared her ass, nowhere near ready to stop.

I held back, going slowly at first until it had adjusted to the girth of my dick, before speeding up my movement. I reached forward and found her dripping wet pussy, fingering her clit while I fucked her ass. She moaned like a whore, pushing her ass back to meet me, the dull thud of the headboard against the wall making me grin.

The hot little bitch on the other side had to know what was going on. I imagined her touching herself, wishing it was her taking a pounding from my cock. One day . . . one day I was going to have those bee-stung lips around my cock. I was going to have her cum on my tongue. I was going to fuck her blind. She needed someone to teach her a lesson. I just had to wait, be patient. The time would come eventually when I could go after what I *really* wanted.

Revenge.

My head nearly exploded. I closed my eyes and filled Bianca's ass with my cum. I grinned. The Scandinavian beauty passed the test. She could stay.

Two hours later, with Bianca sprawled across the bed, passed out after I'd fucked her relentlessly, I collapsed into a heap on the mattress and fell into a deep sleep.

*****

Bianca complained that her pussy was sore and her thighs raw. I grinned, not in the least surprised after the way I'd ravished her over the last week. We showered and went downstairs for breakfast; I'd given her a t-shirt of mine to wear and a pair of silk boxers. It was mid-morning and Mom had gone to her yoga class, so we had the house to ourselves for a few hours.

I had no idea where Maya was; she hadn't appeared since we'd been up and I was beginning to wonder if she was even home. I'd seen her hanging around the house with her friend Quinn over the last seven days, and she'd given me a hard time whenever I'd bumped into her.

Taking Bianca by the hand, I lead her to the pool area, a bottle of orange juice and two towels under my arm. We lazed on the deck chairs, soaking up the sun and dozing off to make up for the sleep we didn't get the night before.

I woke from a sun-dazed sleep when ice cold water hit my overheated body. The shock made me sit upright, my heart beating like it wanted to jump out of my chest.

"Fuck!" I yelled, pissed. Then I saw her. Maya was swimming laps, long arms slicing through the water gracefully. Bianca was still fast asleep, her skin turning pink from overexposure to the sun. Somehow Maya's splashing had hit only me. I got up to open the overhead umbrella, still managing to keep my eyes on the dark head moving swiftly through the water.

About ten minutes later Maya emerged from the pool, her long, lean body covered by the same white bikini I'd seen her in before. The way she stood, it was completely transparent, showing every bit of her pink flesh through the wet fabric. Christ. The cock I'd thought was done for the day hardened to a six on the diamond scale.

My mouth fell slightly open as I took in the hard nipples, the goose bumps on her skin, and her slit as the bikini bottom pulled up between her pussy lips. Camel toe had never looked so good.

My heart slammed against my ribs. Maya looked straight into my eyes and smiled as she shook her hair, her tits jiggling as she moved her body from side to side. I was going to lose my shit any moment.

Before I could react, she reached back and untied her bikini top, letting it drop to the floor. Then she stepped out of the bottoms until she stood dripping wet and completely naked in front of me. All the breath in my lungs expelled in one whoosh. I'd never seen anything so beautiful.

Frozen to the spot, I watched her lean over and scoop the wet bikini from the grass, her perky ass practically in my face. I groaned. My cock was a ten on the diamond scale; it couldn't get any harder.

I wanted to reach out. *To touch her.* Such perfection was unreal. But I was paralyzed—I couldn't move. Her pearly white teeth glistened in the sun as she grabbed a towel off a chair, wrapped it around her body, and walked off into the house.

What. The. Fuck?

If it weren't for my painfully hard cock, I'd think I'd been dreaming.

Chapter 5
MAYA

"Are you telling me you actually just stripped in front of Oliver and then left him hanging with a hard-on?" my best friend Quinn asked. I'd called her as soon as I'd come back inside because I needed her opinion on this. After all, she was the one who suggested it.

My cheeks burned. "Yes."

"Shit, Maya, I'm impressed. When I told you to mess with him I hadn't expected you to actually do it." The awe in her voice made me chuckle.

"I'm not that inexperienced," I said, checking out my toenails. They were starting to chip from all the swimming and needed a new color. I'd get Quinn to paint them with the new polish she'd bought the day before.

"I know, but this is Oliver we're talking about. The encounters you've had are with guys our age. Oliver's in a whole other league."

I shrugged. *Oliver's completely in a league of his own.*

"Yeah, well, I'm pretty sure for the first time ever I managed to fuck with his mind, so kudos to you for giving me that advice."

Images of Oliver sitting on that lounge chair, stunned into silence, flashed through my mind. His hard-on clear for all to see. I'd had him right where I wanted him. But for what? He was hardly going to touch me. No, Oliver simply liked to torment me, and that fact alone made me question why I even wanted him to touch me.

What's wrong with me? I was so screwed up to want him in that way.

"So what's the next thing you're going to do to him?" she asked, as if I had this all figured out in my mind when in reality I had no clue what my next step would be. We'd discussed all the evil things he'd done to me over the years, the way he'd repeatedly humiliated me, and she'd come up with the idea to get back at him by torturing him this way.

I lay back on my bed and twirled my hair in my fingers. "What do you suggest?"

She remained silent for a moment. "Um, how far are you willing to take this? Do you want to sleep with him?"

I groaned. Of course I wanted to sleep with him. But I'd never admit it, not even to my best friend. I was struggling to be honest about it with myself. Sometimes I truly hated him so much I wanted to kill him. "He's shagging that blonde bitch with the big tits, remember? He doesn't even look at me."

"Shit, you just need to get rid of your virginity already. Maybe you could take advantage of him for that. I bet Oliver King could teach you a thing or two."

Yeah, why am I holding out? Most of my friends were screwing their boyfriends, so what was I waiting for?

My core clenched at the thought of Oliver fucking me. I'd fooled around with a couple of guys from school, but somehow I just couldn't bring myself to let them go the distance. While I'd had a few orgasms, none of the guys were as experienced as Oliver. Just the idea of being fucked by a man who knew exactly what he was doing got me wet.

Who was I kidding?

The idea of *Oliver* fucking me got me wet.

Oh God, I really was dirty.

"I don't want to give him my virginity," I said after a few moments of silence, not entirely convinced I'd spoken the truth, but not willing to consider that my deepest desire involved sleeping with Oliver.

"Why are you hanging onto your v-card, Maya? God, you've got guys panting after you, desperate to get in your pants."

I sighed. She'd never understand. Quinn had given hers up a year ago. She was the kind of girl who was completely comfortable in her sexuality, whereas I wasn't. I struggled to believe any guy would truly want me. *The real me.* Why would anyone choose to love me when I had nothing to offer him but flaws? I was so screwed up.

"I'm waiting for the right guy," I lied. It was easier to tell her this, especially as she couldn't see my face. Usually she could read me and it was impossible to lie to her. But I just couldn't explain it to her. Hell, I couldn't even understand it myself.

She didn't need to know that in my mind the *right guy* was none other than my darling stepbrother. In my imagination we were perfect together. If that ever translated to real life, we'd be off-the-charts hot together.

In a sick and twisted way I was saving my virginity for *Oliver*. How could I admit that to anyone?

Quinn bought the lie and moved the conversation back to *Oliver*. "Okay, so sleeping with Oliver is out of the question. I vote you keep teasing him. Push him to his breaking point and then maybe you'll be able to turn the tables. You need to get him eating out of your hand and then tell him to fuck off and leave you alone for good."

I wasn't convinced her plan was the best way forward. Oliver was smart.

He'd see right through me and then where would I be? On top of that, I wasn't sure I had the confidence to pull it off. Not with Oliver. The man unnerved me. I hated him. I wanted him, but I hated him.

Oh God, I dreamt of him.

His hands on me.

His naked body on top of mine.

His mouth. Everywhere.

I pressed my thighs together and took a deep breath. My arousal pulsed between my legs, reminding me how dirty I was. I had to stop thinking of Oliver this way. It was so very wrong.

"No, I think I actually need to stay as far away from him as I can, Quinn. It's safer that way."

"Suit yourself, but I'm telling you, Oliver King wants you. I watched him at the barbeque on Sunday and at dinner last night and I've seen the way his eyes follow your every move. He gets all antsy when you're around, and I've seen how hot you get him just by being in the same room as him. He might treat you like shit, but that's just a cover. The man has it bad."

She was so wrong.

Oliver King hated me and took every opportunity to let me know.

Chapter 6
OLIVER

I was starting to think I'd imagined the whole thing at the pool. Maya avoided me, staying in her room or slipping out when I didn't notice. I hung out with my friends, went to parties, or invited them back to the house where we'd lie around the pool drinking beer, cranking up the music, and working on our suntans. Sometimes the beer went to our heads and we'd be totally juvenile and make idiotic jokes to pass the time.

Bianca was unofficially my girlfriend and I definitely didn't mind that I had a voluptuous blonde in my bed every night. The sex was phenomenal; she was something of a nympho and was always ready for anything I wanted. We'd found a copy of the Kama Sutra in the library and tried just about every position in the book, even the ones that seemed impossible.

I screwed her every which way, trying to fuck the seething rage out of my body and my mind. But it seemed as if nothing helped. The anger stayed. The need remained. Nothing really satisfied the hollowness inside.

I'd found out from Mom that *the kid* had a boyfriend and that she was staying over at her friend's house a lot lately.

"That girl thinks I'm stupid. She thinks I don't know that while she's pretending to be at Quinn's house, she's probably sleeping at her boyfriend's place. But I'm not going to stir up trouble with Alec. It's not my damn problem what she does. Alec will have to deal with it if the girl gets pregnant," Mom said, crossing her arms over her chest. There was no love lost between those two.

The thought of my stepsister with another boy shouldn't have worried me, yet it was constantly on my mind. I found myself wondering how far she'd let him go, if she'd let him taste her, or finger her, or *fuck* her. Kids these days started young. I had no illusion about what went on—I'd been a horny-as-fuck teenager just a few years ago myself and I'd screwed any girl who was willing to spread her legs.

Maya was far from innocent. Flashbacks of that day in her bedroom and at the pool still ran on auto-play in my mind. Shit. It still managed to get me hard just thinking about it.

Because the little prick Maya was chatting to happened to be the same age as her, nobody blinked an eye. For fuck sake, I had to sit through dinner a few times watching her father just shrug and laugh when she hadn't turned up, yet again, saying it was cute that she'd found her first love. Cute? Really? *Not.*

Reluctant to hear more about what Maya was up to, I sat there pretending to be calm while the fire burning in my gut made it unbearable to digest the thoughts, never mind the food. I needed to be indifferent.

On the occasion that she did bother to show up for dinner, she usually brought her friend along too. Quinn gave me the creeps. I'd catch her watching me with an amused expression, her gaze sharp as she sized me up. Why I felt she was constantly judging me, I had no clue. She'd never flirted with me or shown any interest, which was just as well. Although she was pretty, she just wasn't my type.

I'd learned from my friends who knew her that she was a year older than Maya and apparently not too shy to go all the way with guys. I had an uneasy feeling that she was a bad influence on Maya. I'd have to keep my eye on her, ensuring she didn't stir up trouble and push Maya into situations she wasn't quite ready for.

Then there was my mother. Secretly she was pleased that the competition for her husband's attention was out of the house most of the time. A pure narcissist, she wanted to believe she was still the fairest of them all. She'd gladly hand her stepdaughter a poisoned apple and see her fall into a deep sleep, just like in the fairy tale.

The fact that Maya was only sixteen didn't seem to worry anyone, including her father. As long as the boy she dated was from a "good family" everything was okay. *Like hell.* It wasn't okay with me. *Somebody* had to protect her from herself. Wasn't that what family was for?

I shrugged. It really wasn't any of my business and I wasn't sure why the hell I let it bother me. I had my own damn life to live.

I was here for my mother's party and to have a good time. Nothing else.

Chapter 7
MAYA

Nobody had warned me that growing up was this hard to do. Thrown into a world of period pains, out of control hormones, and boys groping at my body at every opportunity was something I wished I'd known about before it happened. Larissa and I never spoke about anything remotely related to sexuality and I didn't feel comfortable discussing these issues with Daddy.

I'd gone from a bright, sunshiny kid to a confused and bewildered teenager. Neither child nor woman, I wasn't sure where I really fit in. Daddy had become busier at work and spent most of his free time with Larissa, and I mourned the loss of the close relationship we'd had before my stepmother and her son changed our comfortable lives forever. There was no going back to the way things were—just Daddy and I—and I missed that closeness and familiarity we'd once had.

With every passing birthday I missed my mom more. Wondering what it would be like to have her hold and comfort me and tell me that everything would be okay. To have her tell me about boys and what was happening to my body. To share my dreams with her and have her believe in me.

I was floundering—struggling with my desires and sexuality.

That's why when Quinn came into my life she was just what I needed. Her parents had just divorced and her mom relocated to our side of town just after her fifteenth birthday. Ever since we'd been tight, covering one another's backs in every situation. I trusted Quinn with my life. Although she was only a year older than me, she had an old soul and was smart and wise—at least in my opinion.

Luckily she had a great relationship with her mother, so she had a handle on most of the facts. But sometimes we had to Google shit to find out more than what her mother was willing to tell her. Like what a real penis looked like. Shit, it was seriously the ugliest thing I'd ever seen. We'd seen pictures of girls our age taking an erect dick into their mouths, but when Quinn found a girl doing it on YouTube I nearly puked. I was sure I'd gag if I ever tried that.

Except if it was Oliver's dick. Knowing that bitch Bianca took his cock in her mouth had made we want to try it, too. Jealousy flooded my insides, making my mouth water at the thought of Oliver's dick between my lips.

Oh God, I'm dirty for having these thoughts about my stepbrother. Shame washed over me and I felt like such a whore that I didn't even tell Quinn about my fantasies.

"Shit, Bee, I don't have anything to wear to your stepmother's party tonight. Can I borrow one of your dresses?" she said, eyeing me for my reaction.

A pang pierced my heart. Whenever she called me "Bee" it immediately reminded me of Oliver. Not that he was ever far from my thoughts anyway, but it just made my heart ache in a strange way. I'd asked Quinn not to call me that, but when she got really excited, like now, she just automatically switched from Maya to Bee.

That was one little cartoon bee I really wanted to hate. I never would've believed how a fictional character could affect my life. Daddy had told me my name meant "generous" in Old Persian and "love" in Nepali and I'd always loved my name.

Until junior high school I hadn't minded being called Maya the Bee. Kids could be cruel and some of my friends had copped it far worse than me. Gabriella had become "Garbage" and it ate at her self-esteem, even though I kept reminding her that it was only stupid twatwaffles who called her that name.

And then Oliver started calling me "little bee." Deep down I loved that he had a special name for me. Lately I couldn't hear the word "bee" without thinking of Oliver and how much he confused me.

Misunderstanding my long pause before answering her, Quinn pulled a face at me. I snapped out of my Oliver haze. "Only if you help me pick out something sensational. I have first dibs."

"Fair enough. Let's see what you have." She opened my closet and raked her hand over the small collection of dresses that hung there with their tags still on them. She whistled through her teeth when she came to the lacy red dress. "Shit, Bee, I wish I had a father who just gave me his credit card to go shopping. You're a lucky bitch," she grinned at me.

"Yeah, it helps the guilt complex that comes with neglecting me since the day he married Larissa. Every once in a while I splurge on dresses I know I'll never wear, just to help him out with that."

"You're strange, you know?" she said, tilting her head to appraise me.

I laughed. "Yes, I do know. But that makes two of us and that's why we're such good friends."

"Exactly. It takes one weird bitch to know another," she laughed. "No wonder I love you as much as I do."

"Hey, stop this fluffy stuff. You're going to ruin my damn make-up if I cry, and it's taken me an hour to get this eyeliner perfect."

"Try on the red one. That color is perfect with your dark hair and bronze skin. I can't imagine wearing red myself, it just screams *look at me*."

I laughed. "So it's okay if everyone looks at *me*?"

She raised an eyebrow and tapped her chin with her index finger, giving me that knowing look that she was on to me. "Hmmm . . . well, correct me if I'm wrong, but I was thinking there was one person in particular whose attention you wanted. So I'm saying dazzle the shit out of him and wear the red one."

Sitting on the edge of the bed, I sighed, shrugging. I didn't know why I was so bothered. "Bianca will be there and she'll make sure Oliver is occupied. He wouldn't notice me even if I went naked. So far my best attempts at stirring him up have failed. He just glares at me."

"Ahhh, but I have a genius plan." The wicked grin on her face and the glint in her eyes didn't bode well for me. I groaned. Lately all of Quinn's plans had backfired, and I was seriously starting to doubt her wisdom, but that didn't stop her from coming up with new ideas.

"Make him jealous. Kiss another boy. Isn't Calvin coming with his parents? Larissa and his mom are friends, aren't they?"

My eyes brightened. I'd had a thing for Calvin once, before Oliver came into my life and ruined me for anyone else. And everyone at school already thought Calvin was my boyfriend, so maybe there wouldn't be any harm in playing along and giving it a whirl. Maybe if I *really* kissed another boy deeply, let his tongue fuck my mouth, I'd like him so much that I'd get over this ridiculous crush I had on my stupid stepbrother. The more I thought about it, the more I liked the idea of it.

"I can kill two birds with one stone," I said, looking forward to executing my plan. Calvin had been drooling all over me in class lately and I knew he would love to have me alone somewhere all to himself. All I had to do was make sure Oliver saw it happen; Calvin would do the rest. He was horny as fuck last time I danced with him at a party, so it wouldn't be difficult to stir him up.

"Oh boy, this is gonna be fun!" Quinn rubbed her hands together, grinning widely.

I eyed the red dress again. It was the sexiest of all the dresses in my closet and I didn't think I'd wear it until I was much older. But desperate measures were needed, and I was going to go all out and take a wild risk.

Quinn chose a deep blue dress for herself that looked better on her than it would have on me. "Wow, that one really suits you. I think you should have it."

"Don't be silly, Maya. I asked if I could borrow it for tonight; I don't want it forever."

"Well maybe you'll change your mind. Guess who else is coming tonight?"

She sucked in a sharp breath. "Who?"

"Our neighbors and their drool-worthy son. Larissa invited them. I heard her talking to his mom earlier confirming that they'd come over since they're new to the suburb and don't have many friends out here."

Her mouth gaped open as she stared at me. "And you're only telling me this now?" she shrieked. "Shit, I'll be his *special* friend."

"Thought I'd keep it as a surprise," I said dryly as she grabbed hold of me and started waltzing around the room like an idiot. "Don't make it too easy for him, okay? Make him work for it."

She laughed. "That depends. If he makes me horny enough, and I'm sure he will, I can't deny myself a taste of his delicious body. You are so lucky to have such a hot neighbor. It's such a damn waste on you. If I were you, I'd stop crushing on Oliver and make out with the new guy."

You aren't me.

"You're in luck, because frankly he does nothing for me. Nobody does to my insides what Oliver does." Boy, was that the truth.

Quinn scrunched her nose. "Honestly, I don't know what it is you see in Oliver. He's obnoxious, rude, and fucking moody. And those are the nice things."

I chuckled. She was spot-on. But she forgot to mention that he was gorgeous and had a sculpted body like I'd never seen on any man.

Slipping into the red dress, I trembled as Quinn did up the zipper. It was so tight I had to suck in a breath, releasing it slowly until I filled into the dress. I still felt naked. The lace plunged into a deep neckline, showing my boobs to perfection. And it was short. So short that if I leaned over too far, my ass would be on display. Yet I felt good. Sophisticated. Sexy. Grown up.

Quinn had stacked my hair up into a messy 'do with only a few tendrils framing my face and now she held out a red lipstick.

"No babe, that's too over-the-top. This dress is enough to handle for one night. Who knows, maybe it will even help me lose my v-card."

I appraised Quinn as she swirled around, showing off her tight ass. "If the men don't go panting after you they either don't have eyes in their heads or their batteries are flat. That new guy doesn't stand a chance—his tongue and his dick will both be hanging out for you."

Quinn beamed at me and it was my turn to twirl. "Oh my God, Bee. You look stunning. If Oliver doesn't get a fucking hard-on when he sees you, the man's a saint. And we both know he isn't." She burst into a fit of giggles, her hand over her mouth. "Just look at yourself in the mirror. You're a knockout, babe."

Chapter 8
OLIVER

The night of Larissa's fortieth birthday party had arrived. She was a standout hostess and really came into her own when she organized a party. I'd come down a little earlier to help her with last minute arrangements, but everything had been taken care of by a stream of caterers and event stylists, so there wasn't anything for me to do other than pour myself a drink and wait for the party to start.

Since it was a balmy evening and the party would be focused around the pool area, I'd dressed in lightweight beige chinos and a light blue button-down shirt. The sun was setting over the ocean and I took a moment to enjoy the peace and quiet before everyone arrived. Sipping on my beer, I admired the masses of garden lights that had been placed around the area, turning it into a tropical paradise.

I watched the band set up near a makeshift dance floor that had been laid down earlier. Larissa took turning forty seriously. I wasn't a fan of fussy parties, but she had outdone herself and everything looked elegant yet festive.

Slowly people came filtering into the area. Some I knew from my earlier years living in the city, and others I introduced myself to if I bumped into them. Strangely almost everyone knew who I was, even though I sometimes didn't have a clue who they were.

I was leaning against a low wall when two sexy beauties, dressed in barely-there shorts and skimpy tops with way too much makeup on, approached me.

"Hi Oliver, so glad to see you made it. Larissa said you might be here." They introduced themselves as Mary-Jane and Sarah before sitting their asses into two nearby chairs. Sarah was already undressing me with her eyes, but mine kept wandering over the slow inflow of guests.

"Yeah, how can a good son miss his Mom's birthday?" I said, giving them one of the charming smiles I reserved for girls who were hot but not quite my type. They kept chatting to me, both trying to outdo the other in the flirting department. They could've saved themselves the trouble. I had a hard time not looking over their heads to see if I could spot Maya. My gaze kept darting around until I couldn't sit still a minute longer.

Surely Maya wouldn't avoid her stepmother's party. Mom and Alec had come outside and were chatting to a group of friends. I excused myself and walked over to greet my mother. She looked even blonder than usual and I was sure she'd spent a lot of time and money at Tony's salon earlier.

"Hey, Mom, you're looking gorgeous tonight. Happy birthday!" I pulled a small Cartier box from my pocket and handed it to her. Luckily they'd wrapped it in the store because I sucked at anything even vaguely craft-like.

"Thanks Oliver, that's so sweet." She kissed my cheek before unwrapping her gift. With a huge smile on her face, she undid the ribbon, then removed the box's lid. Her eyes lit up when she saw the watch.

"Oh, Oliver, it's perfect." She placed it on her wrist amidst her bracelets and smiled up at me.

"I'm glad you like it. It reminds me of you—dainty and pretty."

She squeezed my arm, her eyes watery. "Thanks, my darling boy."

I cleared my throat and gave her a hug. "It's also so that you aren't late again when you visit me in LA and keep me waiting at Starbucks for an hour."

She lightly swatted my arm and laughed. As punctual as I liked to be, Mom was always late.

"Where's Maya?" Alec asked, looking around for his daughter. At least I wasn't the only one wondering why she hadn't made an appearance yet.

"Maybe she's hiding in the kitchen like she often does when we have people over. Her friend Quinn came over this afternoon, so I know that they're around somewhere," my mom said, shrugging.

"Maybe she's caught up with other kids her own age, honey. I'm sure she finds us quite old and boring." Alec chuckled good-naturedly.

Larissa's back stiffened—she definitely took offense to being called that, even if it was in a joking way. She was the kind of person who preferred me to call her by her first name in front of people.

"Is Bianca coming over tonight?" Larissa asked, changing the subject as she dusted some invisible spec of dirt off my collar.

"She'll be over a bit later. She has a friend's twenty-first going on tonight too, so she has to hit both parties." A sensation of relief flooded me as I let out a breath. It was strange but I really didn't want Bianca by my side. I was far more occupied with wondering what Maya was up to.

"Oh, I hope she gets here safely," Mom offered, being her perfect and polite self.

"I'll ring her later to hear when she's coming over," I said, not really caring if she made it or not.

Getting restless after another half hour had passed and tired of making small talk, I made my way indoors. Besides, the few beers I'd consumed made a visit to the bathroom imminent.

I was heading that way when I heard wolf whistles behind me. I turned to see a blond guy standing with a few other dudes, their gazes glued to the stairwell. Swinging around to see what they were looking at, my stomach dropped to my shoes.

Quinn was coming down the stairs, one by one, in ridiculously high heels. If she tripped and fell, she'd be badly injured. But that wasn't what made my mouth go completely dry. Behind her, glowing like a fucking light bulb, was Maya.

Wearing the shortest piece of fabric anyone was crazy enough to call a dress.

Her long bronzed legs went on forever, and although the heels she wore weren't as outrageous as her friend's, they were still hazardous.

I swallowed hard as I took it all in. The deep plunging neckline, the way the red lace complemented her hair and skin, the way she bit her bottom lip shyly even while her eyes were glistening.

And then BAM, her eyes met mine and she nearly stumbled on the second-to-last step. Before I could move, the blond guy had bolted forward and grabbed her around her waist. Her dress shifted up an inch and I swore I could see her panties. Christ, I was going to have a fucking aneurysm.

I could see the headlines: "Stepbrother dies of heart attack at twenty after seeing stepsister nearly naked in public."

I hoped Alec would take one look and send her back to her bedroom to change. What the fuck was Maya thinking walking around in a dress like that? Every boy in the room was fucking her with his eyes, drool practically dripping from their gaping mouths. I bet every prick was hard. Mine sure was. And it wasn't because I needed to take a piss.

Her friend breezed past me, glaring at me as if I'd done something wrong. I grabbed Quinn by the arm. "Take Maya upstairs right now and get her to change. She looks like a slut."

Quinn lashed out. "Jealous much? Maya is gorgeous and you can't handle how the guys are tripping over their dicks to get to her." She narrowed her eyes and lifted her chin. "My advice to you? If you want her, step up and do something about it. Or else shut the fuck up and mind your own damn business."

Ouch. This little bitch was worse than Maya.

Grinding my teeth together, I dropped her arm and stalked away toward the bathroom. Now wasn't the time to go crazy and draw attention to myself.

The asshole was still holding onto Maya and she was smiling at him as if he was the only guy in the universe. Rage unfurled in my stomach, burning through my veins.

Maya was going to pay. Yeah, she'd be sorry she was flaunting herself to all the boys, not to mention letting that blond prick put his hands all over her. I just hadn't made up my mind how I was going to punish her yet.

After I'd taken a leak, I went upstairs to make a phone call to Bianca. I'd changed my mind about her coming over—I needed her to distract me before I did something really stupid. Like smash in a kid's face.

After the phone rang out the first time, I dialed Bianca's number again. She was so damn clingy most of the time and now that I needed her around, she wasn't answering her phone.

Her voice slurred when she picked up the phone. "Ollie, hey baby," she drawled. Suddenly her whiney voice irritated the shit out of me. But I still needed her there. Her lips around my dick were possibly the only way I was going to get rid of this nausea swirling around in my gut.

"Bianca, are you about to come back here?" My head was pounding with a motherfucker of a headache. I closed my eyes and rubbed my temples, waiting for her reply.

She sounded way out of it. "I'm sorry, baby, but I've had too much to drink. I'm staying over at Melissa's place tonight. It's a really good party—you should've come. Now you're stuck at a boring old people's party and I'm here alone."

Damn. The only other option I had was to go there, but Mom would be upset if I left too early, especially before the toasting took place. At least that's what I wanted to think, because there was also Maya and the red dress I needed to attend to.

Bianca giggled. Turning my attention back to the phone call, I heard other voices in the background. "What's so funny?" I asked, pissed that everyone was apparently having fun but me.

"There's this really cute guy hitting on me. See, you should've been here, baby. Who knows what I get up to?"

"Do whatever you want, Bianca. Screw him if you feel like it. I couldn't care less."

I ended the call. It wasn't that I cared that Bianca might land up in another man's bed. It was the exact opposite, and that baffled me. *If she's my girlfriend, I should care, right?* I didn't. Not in the slightest.

Bianca could bang another man all night long and it wouldn't get a rise out of me. But Maya—

Fuck. If Maya even had another guy touch her—

Grinding my teeth together, my head wanted to explode with pain. I couldn't tolerate my thoughts any longer. I definitely needed another drink. Something stronger this time. I made my way down the stairs toward the bar. Movement in the far corner of the passage to the library caught my attention.

It was Maya and that blond prick. He dragged her by the hand into the library. She giggled, swaying slightly. *Has she been drinking?*

Storming closer, I clenched my fists open and closed a few times. I'd had enough of this bullshit. Teenagers shouldn't be wandering off into the library alone. I was going to grab that boy by the scruff and toss him the fuck out.

As I got to the doorway, I froze in my tracks. The little bastard had his tongue down her throat and his hand on her ass. My eyes widened as his other hand slipped below the fabric of her dress, cupping her breast.

My dick throbbed as I watched him kiss her, clumsily pawing her like she was his last meal. He ended the kiss and moved his lips down her chest, exposing her breast. I could see her hard pink nipple in the dim light. He sucked it into his mouth as his hand slid down between her legs.

Maya let out a long shuddering sigh of contentment. Little slut was enjoying it.

I completely lost my shit. Adrenaline spiked through my body and I wasn't immobilized any longer. Clenching my fists, I stormed in like a raging bull.

"Take your filthy paws off her before I make you wish you were never born," I bellowed. With brute force I pulled him off Maya and planted my knee into his crotch. His dick was so hard it bounced off my thigh as I connected with his balls.

Groaning like a wounded bear, he fell to the ground.

My gaze raked up and down Maya's body, taking in her arousal. She'd let him paw her and was getting all worked up by a kid. With wide eyes she pulled her dress back over her naked breast and righted it around her thighs.

"Oliver," she murmured on a shaky breath. I didn't want to hear it. Didn't want her defending the prick.

And the dress—it had to go before I lost my mind and ripped it off her.

"Go back to your room. And burn that fucking dress—I never want to see you wear it again."

Trembling with anger, I watched her kick off the fuck-me heels. Leaving them at my feet, she ran out of the library, a raw sob ripping through her body.

Chapter 9
MAYA

"It was terrible, Quinn. I felt like a dirty whore. What's happening to me? I used to be such a nice girl—" I hugged my knees to my chin and sat on my bed, pulling my oversized t-shirt down to my feet to cover all of me.

"Hush, Maya. Oliver wouldn't react like that if he didn't really want you. I think his rage shows the exact opposite of how you're reading it. He's so freaking jealous he can't help himself. And he's fuming, sure, but what do you expect after he saw Calvin all over you?"

She had a point there. Thank the Lord it wasn't my father who walked in on us. But then again, it wasn't him I was trying to provoke to see how far I could push him. More than anything, I wanted Oliver to crack, to acknowledge that he wanted me as badly as I wanted him.

The expression on my best friend's face was one of admiration. "By the way, I never thought you'd let Calvin go that far. The plan was to make Oliver jealous by *kissing* Calvin, not to let him dry hump you."

Quinn had a way with words that normally made me laugh. But nothing she was saying was brightening my mood. I decided to tell her the truth. I drew in a long breath before I spoke.

"When I saw Oliver standing in the hallway as I came down from the stairs . . . the way he looked at me . . . God, Quinn, it was as if nobody else existed in that moment. My heart nearly leapt out of my throat and it set my body on fire. So when Calvin started kissing me, I closed my eyes and pretended it was Oliver."

"Okaaay," she said, drawing out the last syllable for a few beats too long, "but you were aware that Oliver was actually standing there watching Calvin kiss you?"

"Um . . . the best way I can explain it . . . it was like an out-of-body experience. Knowing Oliver was watching and then pretending it was him all over me, I don't know, I just got so hot that I got carried away."

"You have it bad, honey. Nearly as bad as Oliver. When will the two of you realize you really want one another?"

I sighed, blinking away the tears that were threatening to overcome me. I turned my head away so that Quinn wouldn't see my face.

I had it bad. Oliver, not so much. He wouldn't be banging Bianca and letting me know about it if he did. Yet there was something in his eyes in that split second that made me doubt everything I thought he felt about me. Maybe there was the smallest possibility that Quinn was right. I just couldn't see it, though. One second that morphed into eternity was not enough.

The red dress of sin lay in a heap at the end of my bed.

"That was a bit drastic—telling you to burn the dress," Quinn said, catching me staring at it. "Does he have any idea how much this scrap of lace costs? The man has no idea, obviously."

"Listen, just take the dress. I'll never wear it again anyway. Not just because Oliver said so, but because I'll always remember the look in his eyes." Despair filled my voice. "He really thinks I'm a whore, Quinn. In Oliver's eyes I'm nothing but a cheap slut. He's never going to want me after this."

A slow smile spread over her face. "You're underestimating yourself, honey. Like I said, his reaction was just fear that you'd want another guy instead of him."

Quinn was smart when it came to men. She had a sixth sense about them. "How can you be so sure?" Damn, I wish I had as much confidence as she did.

"Trust me, okay? I'm your best friend and I don't want to see you hurt. I'd never tell you something if it weren't true. You looked amazingly beautiful—there was nothing wrong with you in the dress. It was Oliver who couldn't handle it. I don't think he knew what hit him. And while he was trying to figure it out, he found out that someone had beaten him to it. Major ego crush there, babe." She laughed. "Know what, I actually feel sorry for the poor sucker. He only has eyes for you; nobody else exists when you're around. I mean, where was Bianca, huh? I bet he didn't even care that she wasn't there."

I crawled between the sheets, tired to the bone. This shit was exhausting. One minute I hated the way he treated me, the next I was turned on as fuck by him. Add to that my raging hormones and I was pretty much screwed.

"Go to sleep, Bee. Everything will look so much better in the morning."

I stretched my arms and yawned. "I guess. Thanks for being such a great friend. I'd be lost without you."

"Night, sweetheart," she said, a smile in her voice.

"Night." I swallowed the lump in my throat and turned onto my side. Please could I have a dreamless night? I was exhausted. When I wasn't dealing with Oliver in reality, he was haunting my dreams.

I just couldn't escape the man.

Did I really want to? The thought of him *not* in my life was scarier than anything else.

Chapter 10
OLIVER

Leaning back against the humid tile, I crossed one leg over my knee and waited. The whole bathroom filled with steam, clouding my vision of the body behind the glazed glass doors of the shower. But what I could see—the silhouette of her lithe body as she washed and rinsed her hair—made my cock so hard that my eyes rolled back in my head. Smiling, I listened to her humming out a tune by Coldplay.

I was somewhere between bliss and agony and she wasn't even aware I was there. After Bianca called and said she had a stomach ache and her period, I knew I wasn't getting any action from her tonight. It was going to be self-service, tugging at its very best, and I had the perfect plan to make it really good.

Moments later the water stopped and Maya stepped out of the shower, turning away from me to find a towel, oblivious to my presence. Taking in her peachy ass, my dick stiffened another few degrees, throbbing painfully and tenting my satin boxers.

"Leave the towel and turn around," I commanded in a husky tone. I wanted to see the water droplets on her tits.

She whirled around. Her voice, high-pitched from fright, rang out in the bathroom.

"Wh—what the fuck? Oliver?"

"Yes, little bee." I chuckled as her mouth formed an "O" and her green eyes widened.

Her arms folded over her chest in an attempt to hide her tits from my intense gaze.

"What the fuck are you doing in here?"

"I thought that was pretty obvious," I said, raising an eyebrow. Clasping my hands together I fought the urge to jump up and lick the water droplets running down her body. "Don't play all coy with me, trying to cover up. You've already shown me your tits, remember?"

"What do you want?" she hissed. Her lips smacked together as she frowned at me.

It's okay for her to flaunt her body when she wants to tease me, but she's protesting when I come back for more? I laughed softly, enjoying every moment of her unease.

"You, my dear, are going to help me out. Make me come." The satisfaction of watching the horror on her face made my balls tighten.

She took a step backward. "Perverted asshole. Why the fuck would I do that?"

"Because I saw that pimply-faced kid's tongue down your throat. And his paws on your tits and pussy. That's why." Riled, heat flashed through me as I remembered the moment I caught her and the guy in the library. "He's also the one you've been calling while fingering yourself."

Her eyes narrowed in on me. "So what? You aren't my father. Heck, you aren't even my real brother. What's it to you?" Shit, little bee's words stung.

"That's exactly my point. Unless you want Daddy to know, you'll do as I say."

"What if I tell Daddy what you're doing first?" Her lips turned up into a self-assured grin. She thought she was smart, huh?

"I'll tell him it's a figment of your overactive teenage imagination. He knows that Bianca's my girlfriend and I'm fucking her. Why would I want anything from you?"

Yeah, why would I?

"Uncross your arms, Maya," I ordered, my patience running thin, "and rub your nipples like a good girl."

Her mouth set stubbornly; her eyes glared at me. I bet she wished she could cast a spell to make me vanish into thin air. Her resistance turned me way on. I wasn't a fan of easy.

"Don't fight me. The sooner you do it, the sooner this will be over."

Her head tilted as she let her gaze drop to my boxers. She swallowed hard when she saw my erection throbbing against the silky material. Her eyes snapped back to mine. Her pupils were dilated, the green of her eyes nearly invisible. Little bee was turned on, too.

Breathless, she whispered, "What do you want me to do?"

"Touch yourself until you come. I can't touch you, but I can watch while I take care of myself."

She sucked in a breath, stiffening her back.

"You sick, evil bastard."

"Yeah, yeah, I know. Nothing new there. Now are you going to do it? My cock is fucking aching here."

A small, nearly unperceivable smile twitched at the corners of her mouth. She closed her eyes and leaned back against the tile, spreading her arms and legs to her sides so I could take in the full view.

The lump in my throat became impossible to swallow.

"Touch yourself," I said, my voice gruff. "Everywhere."

She leaned her head back and placed both hands on her body, starting at her neck, then worked her way down her chest until she cupped her breasts. For someone so young, she knew exactly what to do to drive me wild.

Natural instinct?

She pinched her nipples between her fingers, moaning softly while she screwed her eyes shut tighter. Her body glistened in the dim light. Sweat formed on my brow, my skin growing hot as I watched her lick over her lips.

Breathing hard, I pushed my boxers down, letting my dick free. Gripping it tightly in one hand, I spat on the other and started jerking off slowly, my gaze never leaving her body.

"Finger your pussy," I bit out, my voice strained. "Make yourself come."

Splayed fingers caressed over her ribs, then her soft belly, before they finally hovered over her mound. A bright blush spread over her cheeks and she bit into her lip as her hands trembled while smoothing over her skin.

Fisting my cock tighter, my movements sped up. My eyes were nearly popping out of my head, but I couldn't tear them away. She widened her stance, one hand gliding back to a breast and squeezing as the other pushed between her folds, rubbing back and forth rhythmically.

Transfixed, I watched, grunting as I squeezed my balls, imagining her hands doing the work.

"Jesus, little bee," I ground out, ready to explode. The aroma of her arousal drifted on the humid air to my nostrils, sending my mind into a whirl. I licked my lips as I noticed her juices running down her leg. Christ. I wanted my tongue on her, lapping that up.

"Like this, Oliver?" she murmured, scooping some of the juice up with her fingers and bringing them to her lips. She stuck all three fingers into her mouth, sucking it off.

I was going to have a heart attack. I wanted her so badly I seriously considered just throwing her down on the floor and fucking her. Hard.

Fuck the consequences.

Fuck everything.

I just want inside her.

"Hmmm," she hummed, going back for more. It was fucking pouring out of her.

Holding out a hand, she held her wet fingers to me.

What?

Fuck me.

Her eyes opened and locked with mine. Deadly serious. She knew I needed this.

"Taste me."

I pushed to my feet, holding my cock in a vice-like grip. Her eyes didn't stray from mine; she didn't look down, just kept hers trained on mine.

Maya shuddered when I took hold of her wrist and sucked her fingers into my mouth, licking and sucking on them. She was the sweetest thing I'd ever tasted.

I'd be lying if I said I didn't want more. Didn't want to bury my face in her cunt and lick her dry. Fuck her so hard she screamed my name.

"Shit, I'm going to come," I growled, feeling the pressure build to insane levels.

Her skin was on fire, burning through my fingers. I let go of her arm and took a step backward. She closed her eyes again and plunged two fingers inside her wetness, fucking herself where my dick was begging to go.

Short sharp bursts of breath spilled from her lips as her body convulsed a few times.

"Oliver," she gurgled from the back of her throat, letting her pleasure show on her face. I'd never seen anything more beautiful.

There was no holding back a second longer. Warm cum spilled from my dick, some of it hitting her belly. Trembling, she reached down and scooped it up with her index finger, and then, smiling, brought it to her lips.

"Thank you," she whispered, so softly I wasn't sure if I was imagining it. She sucked the pad of her finger into her mouth, tasting me, a serene smile on her face as her eyes fluttered open.

"Now go, Oliver. You got what you came for." Her voice was barely above a whisper, floating to me as if I were in a trance. Her eyes bored into mine, imploring me.

She was right. If I didn't leave now, I wouldn't be able to move my legs when desire gripped me again. I pulled up my boxers, my cum still on my skin and the bathroom floor.

"Go." She repeated, more urgently this time.

I spun on my heels and left, my legs barely able to carry me out.

My cock was still rock hard, begging me for her sweet pussy.

It was one of the best and the worst ideas I'd ever had.

I needed a shower. I'd replay what just happened over and over in my mind, coming again to the images of little bee, the taste of her on my lips.

And then I had to get the fuck out of this place. I didn't dare even get into that bed tonight, knowing it was only a thin wall separating us. I was so close to the edge that the slightest thing would tip me over.

I'd come for Larissa's birthday and thank Christ it was done. From now on, I'd stay away from the kid with her luscious body and her soulful eyes that stole my mind and my sanity.

It would be so much easier if I were in LA, miles away from her. I'd throw myself into my studies, work like a demon, and forget about my stepsister.

At least I could try.

Chapter 11
MAYA

PRESENT

Muffled voices sounded in the background. My head and wrists hurt like a motherfucker. Why was it so damn difficult to open my eyes? It took all of my energy to force my eyelids open.

Where am I?

White walls, white bedding, white ceilings. So much white.

I'm pretty sure this isn't what heaven looks like—or hell for that matter.

"You're awake." A deep voice floated toward me. Fuck.

Further proof that I'm still alive.

I turned my head slowly toward the sound, and fuck me if the man who inhabited every one of my nightmares wasn't standing there, arms crossed over his chest, t-shirt stretched to hell as his muscles bulged. I swallowed the lump in my throat. The way his eyebrows knit together and his lips pursed as he glared at me made my stomach roil.

Maybe this is hell after all.

"Maya. That was a fucking stupid thing to do," Oliver grumbled.

"Back off," a man wearing a white coat and holding a clipboard warned, "she's been through a lot."

Yeah, you must be the doctor. Tell the bastard to leave me alone.

He had no right interfering in my life. Wasn't he the one who always said we were nothing to one another? I didn't need—or want—fucking saving.

My stepbrother moved forward and took my hand in his, stroking the bandage with his thumb. If I weren't already lying flat on my back, I'd be falling over, stunned that he'd touched me. In all these years, he'd avoided most forms of contact. A shiver ran up my spine as his finger traced up my arm, running alongside the drip.

"You and I need to talk, little bee." The smirk on his lips didn't bode well. If I weren't attached to all sorts of wires, I would've reached out and smacked it right off his face.

The doctor smiled at us. "Since you're family, I'll allow you to stay. I'm guessing she wants to thank you for saving her life," he said, nodding in my direction. "But ten minutes at the most—my patient needs to rest."

Thank him? Fuck no. Not in this lifetime. That asshole was part of the reason I was here and in this state, wrists banded and fucking drips stuck into me. And now—now he wanted to play big brother? What the fuck was going on?

The doctor turned on his heels and left the room.

"Where the hell am I? What hospital did you bring me to?"

"Calm down, little sis; don't get your blood pressure sky high."

"Drop the *little* sis bullshit; I don't buy it for a second. You hate my guts as much as I hate yours. You've tormented me for years, so don't pretend that you care now," I hissed.

He held up both hands, palms facing me. "Ah, you know me too well."

"So why did you bring me here? Why not just leave me to bleed out?" I blinked fast, biting back tears. No way in hell would I let him see how he was affecting me.

He chuckled. "Where's the fun in that? Who would I have left to play with? You're not escaping me that easily. In fact, you're not ever getting away from me."

"Wh . . . what?"

"You heard me." He pulled a chair up close to the bed and sat down. His gaze pierced mine until I lowered my eyes. For the first time I couldn't study my hands like I usually did when I wanted to avoid looking at my stepbrother. "To answer your question, you're in a clinic—one that specializes in helping failed suicide victims." He paused to shake his head and tut.

Right now I hated him with every breath left in my body.

"Does my father know?" I whispered. Cringing at the thought, blood rushed to my cheeks and flooded my face with heat.

He cocked his head and scrutinized my face before answering. "No. I think you owe me some gratitude, or at least some sort of thanks for sparing the old prick the grief of losing both his wife and daughter to suicide."

Letting out a long breath, I closed my eyes. My father would be devastated. I'd do anything to spare him more pain.

"I didn't mean to cut so deep. I . . . um." My throat thickened and I could hardly speak.

"How long have you been self-harming? By the cuts on your arms and legs, it's been going on for a while. Why would you, of all people, do such a stupid fucking thing?" His voice was hard and cold. "I thought you were smart, Maya." The accusation in his voice cut deep. Nearly as deep as the blade. "I don't like what you're doing to your perfect little body."

Perfect little body?

Of course he'd seen my damn legs when he found me. I was in my underwear—the sexy shit I'd bought online.

I shrugged. "It's complicated," I said softly, keeping my eyes shut. An asshole like him couldn't ever understand. I wasn't going to waste my breath trying to explain. The main thing was that Daddy never found out. But knowing Oliver as I did, I also knew his silence was going to cost me dearly.

What would he blackmail me into doing this time? Over the years he'd made me do all kinds of stupid things when he found out something about me that I didn't want my father to know. Like the time he made me polish his shoes and make his breakfast every morning of winter break when I was thirteen. And I'd never forget the night in the bathroom after he caught Calvin Jones kissing me, his tongue down my throat at Larissa's party. It was the first time Oliver really went too far.

It wasn't so much that he made me do dirty things for his pleasure that messed me up—deep down I was ready for that and I wanted it as much as he did. No, that wasn't what made me buy my first set of blades.

It was the fact that he left immediately after and didn't come back for two years. Two long fucking years. That's what fucked with my mind.

He'd left—just like Mom—abandoning me and leaving me behind with fucked-up emotions that I didn't have a clue how to deal with. Without any explanation. How did he think I would take that after everything he'd said and done?

He thought it wouldn't affect me? Idiot.

Yeah, I hate him—despise him. Yet I *ached* for him.

In my body.

In my heart.

In my fucking soul.

Ached so fucking much it was more painful than any cutting I'd done.

I sighed, a long, slow breath expelling from my lungs. "What do you want?"

"This time I want something different from you in exchange for my silence. Plus I saved your life, you know. You owe me something extra special for that."

"What?" *Oh God.*

He drew in a long breath but didn't speak. My eyes fluttered open and I watched his handsome face as different emotions flickered in his dark eyes. Eventually his gaze locked onto mine. I sucked in a shuddering breath at what I saw there. Lust. Raw, carnal lust. I'd seen it in his eyes before, but never as intense as this. Oliver's usual brown orbs were nearly black, his pupils fully dilated. It scared the shit out of me. The blood drained from my face and a cold shiver shook my body.

This isn't good.

I waited, holding my breath for what felt like an eternity. His hand closed over mine.

"I want you. Your body."

My mouth dropped open. "*Oliver.*"

His voice was hoarse and low. "I want sex. Whenever. However. No arguments."

Sex?

Sweet Lord, my head was spinning. My core clenched the way it had so many times before when I'd lain in my bed and touched myself while thinking of my stepbrother. The chiseled body he wasn't shy to parade around the house wearing only boxers that sat low on his hips, the deep V that cut into the sides of his groin, the dark hair leading south. Shame and desire washed over me, my heart beating like a drum.

Dirty.

Illicit.

Forbidden.

I was wrong after all. I had died and gone to hell. And my stepbrother was the devil himself, showing me the way to burn for eternity.

Before
Maya's 18th Birthday

Chapter 12
OLIVER

THREE DAYS AGO

The special ringtone I'd selected for my mother's calls sounded out. I brought the phone to my ear. "Morning, Mother. Trouble in paradise?" I asked sarcastically, pinching the bridge of my nose.

She sighed, long and deep. "Oliver, quit it. You have no damn respect for me. I'm your mother, remember?"

I wasn't getting into that conversation with her. "What do you want, Mom?" I asked, softening my tone. I loosened the tie around my neck and undid the top button. Lately she'd started borrowing money from me for what she called "maintenance." I'd been oblivious to how expensive cosmetic procedures were until I started paying for them with my own inheritance. She promised to pay me back, but I knew full well she never would. That would mean she had to explain to her husband why she still needed liposuction and botox and face lifts.

Turning onto my back, I stared up at the ceiling fan as it slowly rotated around its axis. I spread my arms and legs wide on the bed, taking up all of the empty space around me. Living alone in a condo in Los Angeles wasn't all it was cracked up to be.

"Maya's eighteenth birthday party is on Saturday. Alec has asked me to throw a party for her. I know its short notice, and only three days away, but you've just finished your degree and I know you're on a break. Alec wants you there too. Will you please come and at least try to behave properly towards him?"

I sat up in bed. This was just what I needed. An excuse to go to the house. Not that I really needed a reason to visit my mother, but we'd drifted further apart over the last two years and it just felt awkward. Larissa came to LA every three months and we'd catch up then. She had things to do here—like her secret surgeries or botox touch-ups—so she'd tell Alec she was coming to check on me since I'd refused to go to Santa Barbara.

My dark obsession with Maya had finally caught up with me. I'd tried everything to stay away. Fucked countless women in the hopes of finding someone who would quench my thirst for her. Replace her in my mind. They never did—not even close. I'd stopped bringing them home. They were just an endless succession of faceless tramps, each one as forgettable as the last.

"Yes, I'll come up today. I have a few weeks off between graduating and starting my new job. I need some rest anyway." It was true; I'd written my final exam last week and I was still catching up on sleep.

"I'm so proud of you, Oliver. You deserve a break after studying so hard. And you haven't been here for nearly two years. I miss you." She took a deep breath and then sighed. "Seems like I only get to see you when I come to LA. Don't make me throw a damn party just to get you to come home," she chided. "It's less than a two hour drive, you know."

Guilt rolled through my gut. Yeah, I'd been avoiding that place for more reasons than one. "Anything you need me to bring from LA?"

My mother laughed. "No, just bring yourself . . . and your girlfriend if you have one?"

"Nah, lately I sleep alone. Women wear me out and cost a fortune to feed and entertain."

"Oh. What happened to Bianca? I thought the two of you made such a beautiful couple. She'd make beautiful babies, Oliver."

"Jesus, Mom. Bianca's not a breeding mare. I still see her sometimes—she's in Denmark now for a family problem. She'll be back in a few days."

The truth was that I hadn't thought of Bianca since she'd left. Strange how I didn't miss her for a second. Sex was sex in my book. Didn't matter much who the pussy belonged to as long as she made it worthwhile.

There was only one pussy that really taunted me—even in my fucking sleep. I'd wake up with my cock in my hand, jerking hard to dreams of sliding in and out of Maya. I'd come all over the sheets, whispering her name even as I woke to reality.

Two years of staying as far away as possible hadn't changed a fucking thing. If anything, it made it worse. Much worse. She was all I thought about most of the time.

My fascination with my stepsister had grown to fever pitch. Maya drew me to her in ways I didn't like. Yet no amount of fucking, jerking off, drinking, or even time apart could obliterate her from my brain.

I'd lie in bed at night and trace the outlines of her face in my mind. Every outline, every curve, was burned into my memory. Her face. Her body. Her lips. And those fucking eyes. Those eyes that could pierce my soul.

The gravitational pull was too strong. I couldn't stand this situation any longer. I had to go there. Do something about it before it ate me alive. If she was turning eighteen, she was legal.

About fucking time.

"Does Maya have a boyfriend?"

I didn't want to know how many boys had fucked her. Dipped their cocks into the sweet honey pot. The irony was it was okay for them to do so; society would turn a blind eye. Yeah, we lived in a fucked-up world sometimes. Because if I came anywhere near her—not only was it deemed "immoral" just because my mother was married to her father, even though we weren't related by blood, but on top of that I was a man four years older than her. In the eyes of society, I was screwed. I couldn't have the one thing I wanted most.

It was time to change that. Time to find out what my chances really were.

"I'm not sure. She was seeing someone recently but I think they broke up. She doesn't talk to me about her love life."

Suddenly my mood brightened. I was looking forward to taking a shower and driving to Santa Barbara. But not before I went shopping for a special birthday gift for my stepsister.

I made a quick call to Joyce to place an order for what I wanted and then went to get cleaned up and pack for my trip.

Two hours later, I drove to a cake shop down the road from where I lived. I'd always had a sweet tooth and I craved sugar when I studied late into the night; since Joyce had been working there all those years, she knew me pretty well. I'd called her ten minutes earlier to confirm that the cake was ready for pick up and was pleased when she said it was waiting.

"Oh, it's so sweet you're getting a cake of Maya the Bee for your little sister," she cooed as she took my money and rang up the register.

"Yeah, she'll love it because her name is Maya," I said, smiling.

"As per your request, I haven't placed candles on the cake. We sell candles separately if you need some?" I chuckled. Salespeople were the same everywhere—always eager to make an extra sale.

"Sure," I said, nodding once.

"We have boxes in packets of ten." She turned away toward a shelf to find them. "What color?"

"Black. I need eighteen candles, so give me two boxes."

She swung around, the look on her face priceless. "Your little sister is eighteen?" Her mouth hung open and her eyes widened as she stared at me.

"Yep. In three days." I struggled to keep a straight face.

"I . . . I thought she was still a child," she said, looking at the cake and then back at me as if I was crazy.

"We have this little joke between us. I call her *little bee*."

Her face brightened up. "Oh. That's sweet. You're such a great big brother," she said, smiling widely.

Yeah, I am. I'm such a fucking great brother that I obsess about my little sister all the time, wondering what it will be like to fuck her and make her scream.

*****

A few hours later I pulled up at the house. The roses in the front garden had grown to maturity, their fragrance filling the air as I walked up the path to the front door. Since I had my own key, I let myself in, carefully carrying the cake into the dining room.

I smiled as I remembered the look on Joyce's face when I paid for the cake. But it would be nothing compared to the look on Maya's face. I couldn't wait to see her reaction. Hopefully she'd get it and not lose her shit because I got her a birthday cake meant for a child. Maya used to have a much better sense of humor when she was a young girl. The older she got, the less I saw that side of her.

Sometimes I kinda wished I wasn't such a douchebag when I was younger and we could've started on a different foot. But how in the hell was I supposed to know that she'd grow up into such a stunner, or that my dick would have a mind all of its own where she was concerned? Sixteen-year-old boys—the age I was when Maya first came into my life—were clueless. Maya at sixteen was far more mature than I was at the same age. I couldn't wait to see her now that she was nearly eighteen.

Snapping back to the moment, I placed the cake on the table before I went in search of the occupants of the house to announce my arrival.

Mom had warned me that she was going out to get her hair done. Thank fuck she hadn't asked me to pay for her hair maintenance too, because it seemed like she was at the hairdresser just about every other day.

She'd also said that everyone else was busy getting organized for the party later in the evening. Apparently Maya had gone shopping with her best friend to buy a new dress and would be back much later, and Alec had to work as usual. Not that I was surprised, because the way my mother blew through money, the man needed a serious income to support her in the way she liked.

"Hey, anybody home?" I called out. Met with silence, I grabbed my bag and took it upstairs to my bedroom. I had plans to stay for a while. Unpacking my things, I quietly hummed to myself as I hung my shirts in the cupboard.

That's when I heard the loud panting coming from across the hallway.

"Yeah, babe, like that," I heard a man's voice grind out.

What the fuck? Was that Mom and Alec doing it? Despite the fact that I never actually asked, she assured me that their sex life was great and rather adventurous. Even so, surely they wouldn't be having sex out in the open? I mean, Mom knew I was on my way there.

I apprehensively padded my way to the bedroom door and listened, hoping to pick up the direction the noise was coming from. Yep, definitely from the staircase. I'd close the door and pretend I was having a nap—no way did I want to witness that shit.

Just as I was about to close the door, a dark head appeared in my line of vision. It bobbed up and down, the moaning growing louder and louder. Fuck me. I plucked the door open and stared into wide green eyes. Maya had just pulled her mouth off some guy's dick and was fisting his cock up and down furiously. She was so busy staring at me that she nearly got an eyeful of cum as the prick who sat on the stairs, his pants around his ankles, spurted his orgasm into the air.

I didn't know if I should be impressed by the perfect projectile of his cum as it landed on Maya's chest, or be pissed off that she was blowing a guy in full view of practically the entire house. She had some mad skills in that department, because the expression on the dude's face was one of pure fucking ecstasy.

Her head dropped as she looked down to the mess on her chest, her shirt open, one breast out of the cup of her bra, the rosy nipple erect and hard. Christ, I even remembered the color of those nipples in my dreams.

Her mouth dropped open, then closed, as if she didn't know if she should say something or not. Clearly she wasn't expecting to see me. The guy turned his head and saw me standing there, arms folded across my chest, steam coming out my ears.

"Dude. What the fuck, man? Show some fucking respect," I roared.

I stormed forward and grabbed him by the shirt collar. "What was next, your dick inside her?" I bellowed, my entire body shaking. Grinding down on my teeth and with the veins in my head throbbing, I pulled the fucker to his feet and punched him in the stomach.

"Oliver, no! Gerard's my boyfriend," she screamed, alarm all over her face.

"*Ex* fucking boyfriend," I shouted, my blood pressure reaching dangerous levels. I'd seen this jock hanging around over the years. The prick was supposed to be her best friend at some point, along with Quinn.

"Get your pants up and get out of this fucking house. And if I ever see your ugly face anywhere near Maya, you're dead meat. According to Californian law, Maya's not legal yet, asshole, so don't make me call the cops."

The guy had the good sense to pull his pants up and zip his dick closed.

"She turns eighteen on Saturday. What's three days?"

Clenching my jaw so tightly that pain shot through my brain, I balled my fists as I glared at him.

"I said out," I yelled. Rage roiled in my gut. With every second ticking by it became more difficult to control myself. I wanted to snap the prick in half. The cocky fucker wasn't giving up. "You aren't even her real brother, so quit acting like you care about her."

"NOW!"

He jumped to his feet and made his way down, nearly tripping over his own feet. At the bottom of the stairs, he stopped and turned toward Maya. He opened his mouth to speak. Jesus, did he have a fucking death wish?

I growled, my eyes bulging in my head, my blood boiling under the surface of my skin.

With his tail between his legs, he left. Prick didn't even fight for her. There was no way in hell he was good enough for Maya. She deserved so much better.

Maya poked a finger into my chest. "I fucking hate you," she yelled. "I wish you'd stay the fuck out of my life, asshole."

"You've said so a few times before," I sneered.

She stormed off to her bedroom and slammed the door shut. The key ground metal to metal as she locked the door. A car engine started up outside and I heard the wheels spin as it drove away.

Bewildered, I stood there. I'd just saved her from a douche bag who would never make her happy and she was mad at me? The difference was this: if Maya were my girl, I'd fight for her. To the bitter fucking end. He didn't. Was I really so wrong in thinking he wasn't the right man for her?

Chapter 13
MAYA

ONE DAY AGO

"Is Gerard coming?" Quinn asked as we surveyed the caterers moving about as they set up for my eighteenth birthday party the following day. Larissa had outdone herself organizing it, which surprised the hell out of me. I didn't think my stepmother gave two shits about me, but if this party was anything to go by, it would seem she did.

"Yeah, he'll be here late though. He has to work and can't get out of it."

She raised her brows and smiled in that uniquely wicked way that meant she was plotting something. "That gives you more time to play with Oliver. I seriously think you should make a move on him. The man is tripping over his dick to get to you."

I looked in Oliver's direction and found him staring at me. No smile, and definitely no indication that he was tripping over himself to get to me. Quinn was usually right when it came to men, but she had it all wrong where Oliver was concerned. He simply continued to stare at me. Actually, it was more like a glare.

And damn if that glare didn't shoot desire through me.

I turned away from him and gave Quinn my full attention again. "He caught me giving Gerard a blowjob the day he arrived and lost it at him. Like *seriously* lost it." The recollection of that moment caused me to tense up, heat rising in my belly. "Damn Larissa for not telling me that Oliver was on his way. I had no clue he was coming and then BAM, I look up into his eyes while I have Gerard's dick in my mouth."

Quinn burst out laughing. I could see how that could be hilarious from her point of view. Not so funny for me. I'd never been as mortified in my life. There I was, imagining Gerard's cock was Oliver's—and giving it my best shot—only to be caught by the real thing. Standing there—*watching*. Sometimes life was fucking cruel.

"Well that tells you something," she said with that smug look she got when she believed she was right.

I shook my head. "It just tells me what I already knew—Oliver is crazy and I hate him. He's always interfering in my business when it has nothing to do with him. I just wish he would leave me the hell alone and go back to his whores."

Her eyes narrowed on me. "When are you going to admit to yourself that you have it just as bad for him as he has it for you? This has been going on for damn years, Maya. It doesn't have to be anything other than sex if that's all you want."

I would die if she could read my mind.

One minute I wanted to have sex with Oliver and the next I wanted to get as far away from him as possible. My thoughts drove me insane some days. It would be a hell of a lot easier if he weren't in my life.

Maybe I should leave.

Run as far from Oliver King as I could. Go to school in another state.

And goddamn it, those thoughts alone twisted my stomach in panic. The thought of not seeing him drove me crazier than he ever could with his taunts. I had two years of experience in exactly how that felt. It sucked.

"Maya? Did you hear what I said?"

Her voice cut through my thoughts. "Sorry, yeah, I heard you. I can't imagine sleeping with him. I don't think my father would approve. Besides, it's just gross thinking of screwing my freaking stepbrother." That was the biggest lie I'd ever told my best friend. I'd rather not admit the exorbitant number of hours I'd spent imagining sleeping with him. I still wasn't any closer to knowing how to handle this.

I'm so damn conflicted between what I want and what I know is right.

She shrugged. "Suit yourself, but I think you two need to deal with this attraction soon. It's consuming you, and I worry about where it'll all end up."

Quinn was right. Oliver consumed my thoughts day and night. But she was dreaming if she thought I would ever go to him and admit any of this.

"Maya." The voice I heard in my dreams floated from behind me and I turned to find Oliver standing behind me.

I shivered under his gaze. Those steely eyes of his pierced my soul and stirred a need in me that I struggled to understand. My legs threatened to buckle under me as the need for him blazed through my body.

As we stood staring at each other, Quinn excused herself. "I'm going to leave you two to it. I'll catch up with you later, Maya."

I watched her go and then found Oliver's gaze again. It hadn't deviated from me. He'd moved closer so our bodies almost touched and his warm minty breath danced across my face.

Close enough to cause me to lose all common sense.

"Is that prick whose dick was in your mouth the other day coming tonight?" he demanded to know, his voice dripping with scorn. "Your *ex*?"

And just like that, any desire for him evaporated, anger settling in its place.

"Screw you, Oliver," I spat.

"You'd like that, wouldn't you, little bee? My cock fucking you, showing you what you've been missing with all those school boys."

I tried to move away from him, desperately needing to put some distance between us. "Don't delude yourself. The last thing I want is your cock."

The vein in his neck pulsed and anger clouded his features. His hand snaked out and grabbed me around the waist, pulling me back to him. "One of these days you'll know what my cock feels like. I'll make you my slut, Maya, and you will fucking beg for it. You'll crave what I can give you."

Every nerve ending in my body sparked with desire and my heart beat so fast it could've jumped out of my throat at any moment.

Oh my God, I had to be sick to be turned on by those words.

But I was.

So. Fucking. Turned. On.

Oliver had flipped the switch again with just those words.

How the hell does he do that?

I tried to struggle out of his hold but his grip tightened around my waist, his fingers digging in hard. The pain shot through me and I begged, "Let me go, you're hurting me."

Something flashed in his eyes. Satisfaction? In some ways he was still a mystery to me, even after six years, so I couldn't be sure. Bending his face closer to mine, he taunted me. "Good. You'll learn to enjoy pain when you're with me."

Fear surged through me. Oliver wasn't making sense anymore and this conversation needed to end. I pulled away hard and he finally let me go. As I stumbled backwards, I snapped. "Stay away from me, Oliver. I'm not interested in you, your cock, or your pain." *Lie. Damn lie.* Without giving him a chance to reply, I turned and stalked out of the room.

I'd always known Oliver King was bad news and this just proved it.

And yet, my core whispered its sick desire for everything he had to offer. My panties were soaked and I bet he knew it.

Not only did I want his cock, I fucking craved it. How much longer could I fool myself into believing I didn't? But I had to resist him—he only wanted me as a plaything. As much as I told myself it was only sex I wanted from him, I knew that once he had me, I'd want more. Always more. And that was just plain fucking dangerous.

No good could come of it. Regardless of how much I wanted it.

Chapter 14
MAYA

THE MORNING OF MY BIRTHDAY

I woke up the same as any other day, but there was something different about that day that set a swarm of butterflies loose in my stomach.

I was no longer a child.

I said it out loud. "Eighteen."

Eighteen.

Officially an adult in most parts of the world. It was a big deal. And yet, I'd had a different childhood than a lot of girls my age, so in some ways I felt a lot older than what I was.

Yawning, I sat up and stretched my limbs out in the queen size bed. My gaze darted through the window and rested on the pair of birds in the tree outside, as had become my morning ritual. They'd built a nest and laid three eggs. I'd been watching closely and waiting for them to crack open for days. It was the first thing I did every morning—check if the eggs had hatched yet. Still nothing. Maybe it would happen today. It would be the best birthday present ever.

A pang went through my heart.

If things were different, the best present would've been my mother giving me a smile and a hug. Her telling me she was proud of me. That I'd grown into a beautiful young woman.

I missed her so much that my heart ached. Bonds were formed in the early stages of my life that I couldn't deny in spite of the amount of time that had passed. Sure, they weren't as strong as I would've liked, but they were there nevertheless.

I got up to have a pee and shower and to get ready for my day. It was the one day Daddy always made a fuss of me, and I was looking forward to extra attention from him.

And, of course, Oliver was there too. He'd never been at the house on my actual birthday, so I wondered how he'd act on my special day. If he'd still be so damn mean to me.

My reflection stared back at me from the bathroom mirror.

God, I'm still so young.

I'd filled out physically; my breasts filled a C-cup and my hips were rounder and my ass, of course, was bigger too. But other than that, it was still the same ol' me.

I had so much life ahead of me.

So much I didn't know.

So much more I wanted to experience.

I'd waited for this day for a long time, because I wanted to know what Mom would have looked like when she died. Finally, I was the exact same age as what she was when she took her life. Megan Christina Childs was barely an adult when she left the world.

Overwhelming sadness flooded my heart and reflected back at me. Dull and misty, I stared at the sad green eyes speckled with gold that Daddy said were exactly like hers. I never could quite tell from the pictures of her I'd stared at for hours on end, so I took his word on it.

Was it really that bad *having me at eighteen that she couldn't carry on?* My dad loved her with all his heart, so it couldn't have been that which made her do it. Now that I was eighteen too, I had every reason to want to live, to see what life had in store for me.

It had to be me. It was the only explanation—Mom couldn't cope with having a baby.

ME.

If Megan Childs knew how her actions would affect and damage her baby, would she still choose the same route?

I'd hoped that turning eighteen would help me understand. It didn't. Feeling worse than ever—wretched that I was unable to grasp her internal wounds, her suffering, and her damaging perceptions—I was going to mourn her loss worse than any other day.

I couldn't look any longer—the face I was cursed with had driven a wedge between Daddy and me. As much as I wanted to blame Larissa, deep in my heart I knew it wasn't the full truth of why Daddy avoided looking at me.

Letting out a long breath, I turned away from my reflection. It did me no good. If I could live the rest of my life never having to look into another mirror, it would be a blessing.

Turning eighteen hadn't brought the answers I'd hoped for—it only confused me more. Made me hurt inside. Question my existence.

In the shower, I let the stream of water wash over me, taking a moment to allow myself to cry and let the tears disappear down the drain. I had to shake this morbidity and put on a happy face, because if I wanted Daddy to see me, his Princess Maya, I didn't want him to glimpse my mother in my eyes.

Dressed in my usual attire of shorts and a loose top, I pulled my hair into a pony tail without looking into the mirror and made my way downstairs to face the day with false bravado.

Being the kind of girl who needed breakfast and coffee to start the day, I made my way to the kitchen, hoping I'd be able to enjoy my meal without seeing anyone else as it was still really early. Sleeping without drawing the curtains closed usually had me up before the rest of the household stirred.

Daddy had told me the night before that he'd leave at the crack of dawn to see a few patients and do his rounds so that he'd be free earlier for my party. Larissa was probably still sleeping and Quinn hadn't arrived yet. As for Oliver . . . he was probably sleeping and he rarely made an appearance before midmorning, so it was just me in the kitchen before the bustle started.

I rustled up some scrambled eggs and toast and was just making a mug of steaming java when I heard footsteps behind me. By the way the hairs stood up on my neck and arms, it could only be one person. What was *he* doing up so damn early?

I swung around and slammed into a hard chest. I swallowed my gasp, completely taken off guard. Oliver had never snuck up this closely to me. I hoped he couldn't hear how hard my heart was beating.

"Little bee, good morning!" He smiled down at me, small crinkles forming at the corners of his eyes. Good Lord, what was that cliché about *having me at hello*? It made perfect sense to me now.

"Morning," I croaked, unable to say if it was going to be *good* at this point. Warily I scrutinized his handsome face. The wide smile seemed to be genuine. What was going on? Was Oliver sleepwalking?

His arm slid around my waist and he pulled me inches closer to him. Dazzled, all I could register was Oliver's minty breath floating to me as his mouth moved to speak. "Happy birthday, Maya."

Dipping his head, his lips brushed over mine. Sweet and gentle. My back stiffened. Was I in some sort of dream? This wasn't my stepbrother. Aliens must have taken over his body. Hell, maybe they'd abducted both of us.

"Relax, little bee." His voice was soft and calm, yet the way he pulled me tightly against his chest was forceful and possessive. *Ahhh, Oliver is in there somewhere after all.*

My heart pounded against his chest and I was damn sure his was beating as fast as mine. He pulled his head back and lifted my chin so that my eyes met his. They were soft, kind even.

"I just want to welcome you to adulthood. Wish you a wonderful life."

Leaning in, his lips pressed against mine. Warm. Sweet. Delicious.

Lingering.

My heart wanted to explode. The world stood still; it was only us. I really didn't want to wake from this dream.

After the longest moment—a moment that felt like eternity—he broke the kiss. One hand snaked around my neck, the other pressed me to his chest. Oliver rested his forehead against mine and we stood like that as if we never wanted to move. Afraid to break the spell, I slowed my breathing and just soaked up everything about his closeness. It was surreal. I'd never felt anything like this in my whole life.

It wasn't lust, anger, or hatred. That I was sure of. But exactly what is was, I couldn't say.

Of all the people in the world, Oliver was the first to wish me on my birthday. And it just felt perfect. The way I wished it could always be. Oh God, this was the best birthday present—one I never expected.

"I have something for you. Come." He let me go and instantly I felt the loss of his body so close to mine. His warmth gone.

No.

I want more. Of sweet Oliver kissing me. Holding me as if I would break.

Please, God. I would do anything for more.

I found my voice. "Wh . . .what?" I said, blinking fast as he gifted me with a brilliant smile. It wasn't over yet. Thank you, God!

He grabbed my hand and pulled me toward the fridge. Then he pushed me back onto a stool close by. This wasn't making any sense. I watched as he opened the fridge door and moved a few things from one shelf to another until a pink and black box was exposed. What the hell?

Pulling the box from the fridge with a huge grin on his face, he said, "Close your eyes 'til I say you can open them."

Was there no end to sweet Oliver? Now he wanted to surprise me? Good Lord, my heart could hardly handle it. My eyes fluttered closed. This was fun. This was how I wished Oliver could always be to me.

I took a deep breath as I heard the box shift over the granite top and Oliver chuckle softly. He was enjoying this. Maybe a bit too much? My heart pounded in my throat. What if it was a prank?

"Open your eyes, Maya." His voice was happy and excited. Something I'd never heard before. I couldn't stand the suspense a moment longer. My eyes flew open to look—not at the box, but at him.

"See what I got you? I hope you like it!" Oliver was like a big kid, rubbing his hands together and grinning like a goof. My heart did a summersault. *This man.* The way he was now—

Staying seated as my knees wobbled that much that I was afraid to stand, I leaned forward and peered into the box.

"Oliver!"

"Like it? Tell me you do!" My gaze swung from the cake to his. Oliver's eyes were bright and shiny. He was happy. My heart was going to burst.

"I . . . I do. It's amazing." I wasn't really talking about the cake. It was the expression of joy on his face that I'd never witnessed before that took my breath away. "You got me a cake of Maya the Bee!"

I'd had a few over the years, especially when I was younger. But this one was by far the most precious. It had eighteen black candles, nine on each of the bee's wings.

His eyes were blazing. "There's more. See what's in her hand?" He pointed to a box.

"Wh . . . what?" Why had I turned into a stuttering fool? I leaned over to take another look. In the bee's hand was a small box. I sucked in a breath. How had I not noticed the Cartier wrapping before?

"Open it. I want to see your face."

"You get it," I said, suddenly shy.

"Okay. Hold out your hand, little bee."

I did. Mesmerized, I watched him place the box in my hand. It wasn't that it was Cartier that had my mouth dry and butterflies swarming my belly. It was that Oliver had gone out of his way to get me something special for my birthday.

It was just too good to be true.

Beaming from ear to ear, he placed the box in my palm. I was shaking so much, but I couldn't hide it. Oliver didn't seem to notice. With trembling fingers I pulled at the beautiful bow, almost too sorry to undo such perfection.

I carefully lifted the lid off the box.

Gasping, my eyes fell on the contents. A beautiful necklace, a gold circle studded with what could only be diamonds, lay on the velvet cushion.

"Like it?"

"Oh, Oliver. I love it," I said on a shaky breath, fighting back tears. I'd seen this design in one of my magazines. It was called *the circle of life*.

Did Oliver know that? Was he trying to tell me something? Or was I reading too much into it. *Yeah, I must be.* My mind was in a jumble and I could hardly believe this was really happening to me.

With tremulous fingers I lifted it from the box and held it up to the sunlight streaming through the kitchen window. The way the morning light hit it, it sparkled and made shapes all over the ceiling. I sucked in a breath at the sheer beauty of the magical moment.

"Here, let me put it on for you." Oliver's fingers brushed against mine, sending a bolt of lightning through my arm that spread straight to my core. "I'm glad you like it, little bee." His voice was low and husky. He must've felt it too—the electric spark between us—interpreting it as my excitement about the jewelry.

Bending my head down, I couldn't speak, so I just let him place it around my neck and fasten it at the back. His hands slipped around my neck, both thumbs massaging my nape in small circles. Then, just as suddenly, he pulled away.

I gasped as he swiveled the stool toward him.

"You haven't said *thank you yet*, little bee." His eyes were liquid pools of chocolate. Soft. Beautiful.

I couldn't tear my gaze from his. I clenched my thighs together, feeling the throb grow with each passing moment.

"Thank you, Oliver. It's the most beautiful birthday present I've ever had."

It was true. Nothing would ever beat this.

He took both my hands in his, rubbing my palms with his thumbs. How could such a simple action drive me completely crazy? I wanted to jump his bones, kiss his lips, throw myself at him.

Instead I sat there, staring into those eyes. This was a day of firsts. I only hoped I wouldn't wake up to find it was all a beautiful dream. I reached up to touch the necklace.

"It's called *the circle of life*, Maya. I hope it brings you happiness."

"Thank you," I whispered, my voice cracking.

Oliver swallowed a lump in his throat and nodded.

"And for the cake. It's so sweet of you. I love it." God, finally I had my voice back. "Where did you get it?"

He laughed. "I had it specially made for you. The lady who runs the shop was so shocked when she heard you were eighteen and not eight. You should've seen her face. Hilarious."

We both started laughing.

"Good morning, Princess Maya," Daddy said as he walked through the door. "And happy birthday to my most favorite girl in the world."

He came up to me and pulled me into a hug, then kissed my forehead.

I closed my eyes and shot up a thank you to the heavens. The two men in my life had just made me the happiest girl alive.

Chapter 15
OLIVER

MIDDAY

Since Alec arrived back from his morning rounds with patients, I'd left him and Maya in the kitchen. It seemed as if they needed alone time and I was more than happy to give them that. I'd gone so far out of my normal comfort zone with Maya that I was relieved to get the hell out of there before I melted into a puddle at her feet.

For the first time I'd let my guard down. Let myself be "normal" around my stepsister and opened up more to her than I'd done with any woman. Not that there was normal in my life; everyone knew me as moody and broody and that was the way I liked it. It kept nosy people out of my business. Yet, on a deep level, I yearned for more of what happened between Maya and me.

I'd never known that just seeing a sparkle in a woman's eyes and a sweet smile on her lips could make my heart so damn full.

Stuck with feelings that were so damn foreign to me that they made my fucking head hurt, I went back to my room and lay down on my bed, reliving the moments in the kitchen.

If I had to be honest, Maya's reaction had totally blown me away. I hadn't expected her to go along with it, nor had I anticipated her reaction to my gifts. Knowing that money wasn't an issue to her and that her father gave her practically anything money could buy, I'd chosen her gifts carefully. They had meaning to me, but I didn't expect her to get it that easily. It was as if she just knew. How was that possible? I'd never experienced anything like it and it was driving me crazy; I both wanted more of it and I also wanted none of it.

I pulled a pillow over my head so I could think my way out of this fucked-up situation. I had to do something to put the detachment between Maya and me back into play.

After going round and round in circles, I made up my mind on a course of action. I needed to bring Bianca back into the picture. She'd been moping since I'd ditched her in LA, but I needed a distraction and a shield between Maya and myself before I did something really stupid.

I was going fucking soft. I didn't know what it was about Maya that morning, but I just couldn't bring myself to be the usual ogre with her. And it just felt so damn good that it scared the shit out of me.

Why couldn't we always be like that when we were together? Why did we have animosity between us that drove us both to be ugly toward one another? I wished it could be different, but it couldn't. I had to stay the fuck away from her even if I didn't want to. My control was slipping and it worried me.

I'd always wanted her body. There was no surprise there. But today she pulled at my fucking heartstrings. The one place I let no woman go.

I hadn't expected her to be in the kitchen so early, and when I saw her standing there, waiting for her coffee, she was lost in thought and totally in another place. She looked so damn vulnerable that all I wanted to do was pull her into my arms and tell her everything would be okay.

Maya unlocked a fierce desire in me to protect her and I didn't know how to handle it. She'd reminded me so many times that I wasn't her real brother that it was stuck in my head. But the way I wanted to protect her was more than in a brotherly way. It was man to woman. Ancient instinct kicking in.

Fighting every urge in my body to go to Maya and tell her how I felt, to put this stupid shit between us to rest, I pulled my phone from my pocket. This was the only way I knew how to keep my distance from Maya. By putting Bianca between us. Even though lately the blonde annoyed me more than anything else.

Bianca had just returned from Denmark, and being eager to get back into my bed, it didn't take much to convince her to drive to Mom's house and spend time with me. She was leaving permanently for Denmark in a month's time and had indicated that she was more than willing to let me fuck her sideways before she left.

Two and a half hours later, Bianca arrived. She was still as hot and horny as always, so I took her up to my room and fucked her brains out, not caring about the headboard banging against the wall or Bianca's screaming when she came. The blonde could have been a blow-up doll for all I cared. I had fucking demons to exorcise; it was going to take a hell of a lot of sex to get the image of Maya's face out of my mind.

Images flitted though my head of Maya—all the faces I'd seen over the years. Sucking a guy's dick . . . glaring at me with disgust . . . looking at me with tears in her eyes . . . her expression when she came . . . vulnerable and happy, smiling up at me.

My gut twisted into a tight knot. Of all the faces, it was the one I'd seen that morning that was fucking with my head the most. And her lips when I kissed her. Fuck. I'd never, never, never, felt like that with any chick. Instinctively I knew I never would again, either.

"Hey, babe," Bianca said sweetly as she slid her arms around my waist, bringing me from my thoughts. "You seem so far away. Come back to me. Kiss me, bad boy."

Standing on tiptoes, she tilted her head backward and puckered her lips, waiting for a kiss. I leaned down and covered her mouth with mine, trying my best to get back into her and forget about the girl who was invading my thoughts.

"You're so moody. What's wrong, babe?" she said as the kiss ended.

I pulled away, irritability and the strangest hollowness filling my gut. I needed to cool the fuck down or I'd explode.

"Let's go for a swim," I said, pulling her toward the door and down the stairs. I didn't want to think about Maya for a second longer.

"Slow down, you're going to break your neck," Bianca squealed as we barged through the patio door. She was practically breathless as we reached the pool area.

Letting go of her hand, I dived straight in. My heart nearly arrested from the sudden impact of the cold water. I swam a few furious laps, burning off as much energy as I could. Only after about five minutes did I notice that Bianca hadn't joined me in the pool. She had settled onto a lounge chair and was watching me with a puzzled look on her face.

When I finally emerged from the water, dripping wet and feeling a lot better, I strolled over to where she sat, paging through a magazine. I grinned down at her and shook my hair. Covered with water droplets, she shrieked. "Stop it! You're so mean. My body is all hot from the sun and that's just freezing." Her nipples were hard under her bikini top.

"More reason why you should've jumped in with me," I smirked.

"Not if the water is as cold as the droplets on me," she said, pulling up her nose.

I wiggled both eyebrows at her. "I could've been feeling you up under the water to warm you up. You could've been riding my dick."

She swatted my leg with her magazine. "Next time. I promise."

Lying back on my chair, I stared up at my stepsister's window. Why was I still obsessing over Maya? No matter how hard I tried, I just couldn't shake thoughts of her. Christ, this was doing my fucking head in. I was a grown man of twenty-two and I was thinking more about Maya than of the girl lying right next to me. My fucking head was messed up.

"Babe, come over here," I summoned. "My dick needs attention." Maybe Bianca could distract my thoughts. Fuck knows my cock was hard enough—the cold water hadn't changed anything about that.

She dropped her magazine and gifted me with a wicked smile. "Sure baby, I was wondering when you would be ready for me."

"Get on your knees," I growled. "Suck my dick and make me come."

I need to forget another set of lips. The ones tormenting me. The ones I tasted earlier and want more than anything.

Alarm bells were going off in my head. Maya hadn't resisted me. If I didn't know better, wasn't hundred percent sure that she detested me, I could've sworn she was loving every moment. She hadn't kissed me back, but neither had she fought me off. And the way her eyes shone all the time and her lips trembled still had me hard. I'd felt like a fucking lightning bolt had struck me when I touched her hand, for fuck sake.

Could it be that there was something more than lust between us?

Christ, no. I couldn't let that happen.

Don't confuse lust with something else, Oliver. It's only your imagination. Rein it in, man.

Bianca slid off the chair and kneeled on the grass. She slid her hands towards my wet swimwear and made quick work of releasing my cock. Teasing me with her tongue, she licked up and down my thick shaft before taking the swollen head in her mouth. Leaning back, I closed my eyes as her mouth did its job, her tongue swirling around my cock.

"Suck my balls, babe, then take my cock deep down your throat." I pushed her head down and held it in place, making her deep-throat me until she nearly gagged.

My skin crawled. Someone was watching us. My eyes popped open and zeroed in on where I felt it coming from. *Her* bedroom window.

I sucked in a breath when my eyes clashed with hers. There she stood, covered only in a white towel, her dark hair wet and dripping down her shoulders, watching me with an open mouth. I grinned up at her, so fucking turned on that she was watching that my balls contracted tightly.

"Show me your tits," I said, knowing my voice would carry over the lawn and float up to her. Bianca's head tried to lift, but I held her down with force. "Keep sucking, babe. I'm so fucking close, I can feel it," I hissed at her.

To my utter shock, Maya dropped the towel and pressed her perfect fucking tits against the glass. Her eyes were wild, her hand slipping down between her legs. Christ. As Maya's fingers plunged inside, I came hard, pulsing into Bianca's mouth with brutal force. I fought to keep my eyes open, but they closed of their own accord as I grunted out my orgasm.

Seconds later, my eyes flew open, pinned to the window. Nothing. Just a curtain flapping in the breeze.

Was I losing my fucking mind? Hallucinating?

I blinked fast, my mouth dry as I pushed Bianca away.

"Fuck, Oliver, what's gotten into you lately? You're like a bear with a headache. And your mood swings are driving me crazy."

"It's nothing," I grunted, not in the mood to talk.

Fucking and women talking should be mutually exclusive.

Pouting, Bianca cupped her breasts and squeezed. "What about me, babe? You can't leave me all wet. And I'm not talking about the water, either." In one fluid movement, she straddled my hips, pushed her bikini bottoms to the side and impaled herself onto me. Fuck, she was right. She was wet and warm, riding my cock like a wanton woman. I held onto her hips, helping her up and down. Thank fuck her eyes were closed, because try as I might, I couldn't watch her face.

My gaze was pinned on a window. Waiting for another glimpse of a girl I had no place wanting. Illicit desire burned through my body, craving the tight pussy of the girl who filled my depraved mind.

Disappointment washed over me. Maya wasn't there. As fucking crazy as it seemed I wanted to look into *her eyes* when the woman riding me came on my cock.

Yep, I was losing my fucking mind for sure. I was certifiable.

Obsessed with my stepsister. *I still want her.* What kind of immoral degenerate was I to crave her when I had a perfectly good pussy sitting on my cock?

Bianca came with a loud moan, uninhibited and never being one to hide her enjoyment. But me? I couldn't do it. I couldn't come inside her. Not with my fucking mind elsewhere. I had turned stark raving mad, just like my father. It ran in my genes, and now I knew for certain I was just as immoral and sick as he was.

My plan with Bianca wasn't working. The battle to exorcise my demons was an epic fail. Hopefully I'd succeeded in alienating Maya.

I was a monster. Dark. Depraved.

I wanted what I could never have.

Maybe it was time to admit that my obsession with Maya overwhelmed me. And since that morning in the kitchen it had gotten even worse.

Illicit. Burning like a raging fire inside me.

Two years had changed nothing. *Nothing.*

I wanted my stepsister.

More. Than. Ever.

I needed a new plan. A way to feed my obsession.

Chapter 16
MAYA

EARLY EVENING

Remembering only too well the repercussions of the last party Larissa held, not to mention the red dress fiasco, I stood in front of my closet, unable to decide what to wear to my birthday party. I didn't really care. Flicking through everything I owned, including the new dress Quinn and I bought only a few days ago, I discarded one item after the other. I'd reached that point every woman does—a closet full of clothes and nothing to wear.

My eyes glazed over as I turned away from the closet, leaving the doors wide open, and flung myself onto my bed.

I let out a long, shuddering sigh. It was time I faced the truth: Oliver simply wasn't into me, and nothing I did would change that.

How could I have gone from sad when I woke up, to happy beyond words at breakfast, to murderous in the afternoon? Easy. My stepbrother.

I'd been in heaven that morning when Oliver surprised me with my birthday gifts and was so sweet to me. I was right—it was all a damn illusion. And I hadn't discounted the alien theory either. Right this minute I could easily smash the fucking Maya the Bee cake into his damn face.

After Daddy arrived and broke the special *something* between Oliver and me, I was still a happy girl because my dad had sought me out and made a fuss of me all through the morning. He'd brought me flowers and a beautiful pair of diamond earrings that he wanted me to wear at the party.

But then Bianca arrived by midmorning. I couldn't believe my eyes when she showed up out of the blue. I'd gotten the distinct impression from Larissa that they weren't really an item any longer, but here the bitch was.

Oliver had literally chased my boyfriend out, yet he had his whore back and they had done a fine job taunting me with sex noises and wallbanging until it drove me crazy.

Had what happened that morning in the kitchen meant absolutely nothing to Oliver? Had I just wanted to see the sweet side of him when in fact there was none? How could I be so damn stupid to believe that he actually liked me—no, more than liked me, with the way he'd acted?

I wished my mom was there so that I could rant and rave to her. I'd tried to call Quinn, but she'd turned her phone off. Since she had a part-time job over weekends, she wouldn't be at my house until an hour before the party. It sucked, because more than ever, I needed her to help me get ready.

All the joy had been sucked right out of me. Every bit of happiness I'd felt that morning had evaporated after I'd had my shower and come to my bedroom to start getting ready for the party.

Still fuming about Bianca's arrival and what went on in Oliver's bedroom, I'd taken a step toward the window when I saw the two of them by the pool.

Gutted that Oliver had the bitch suck his dick out by the pool as if he wanted to be seen, I wanted to show him what he missed. I'd decided before Bianca had arrived I was going to give up my virginity to Oliver, that it was time I grew up and stopped being hot and cold toward him. I'd had enough of the cat and mouse games. I was going to tell him how I felt—how much I wanted him—and let it go from there.

But no.

He had to spoil it all by getting his whore to come over.

I'd worked myself up in the shower, remembering the way it felt when he'd pressed his lips to mine, and I could kick my own ass for not having responded.

And so I'd finger-fucked myself out of pure frustration, letting Oliver watch because there was no way he was going to have me after all. And then I flopped onto my bed and cried my heart out. I was the stupidest girl on the planet. I'd let Oliver fool me into thinking he cared about me when in reality it couldn't be farther from the truth. I had no boyfriend, and I certainly didn't have Oliver.

As far as Gerard was concerned, I really didn't care. I'd lost all respect for him the moment he'd actually allowed Oliver to intimidate him. I'd waited for him to challenge Oliver, to put up some sort of fight. Didn't happen. He didn't even bother to stand up to my stepbrother for me. Instinctively I knew that was a bad sign—a guy should want to fight for his woman. Right?

I'd finally passed out from exhaustion and fallen into a fitful sleep, filled with nightmares.

It was nearly dark outside when I woke with a start.

"Hey, can I ask you a favor?" Bianca stuck her head inside the door of my bedroom and brought me out of my funk.

Not moving from the fetal position I was lying in, I eyed her suspiciously. Bitch had hardly spoken ten words to me over the years except when she wanted something. Usually she was so damn wrapped around Oliver she just ignored me.

"Yeah?" I answered, my curiosity getting the better of me.

"When Oliver asked me to come over this morning, he didn't mention your party. Just told me to hurry. I didn't bring anything to wear. Mind if I borrow something of yours?" Her false smile didn't reach her eyes.

I swallowed hard. The gall some people had was unbelievable. She had the whole damn afternoon to get down to a store and buy something. Instead she stayed in Oliver's room banging him and then blowing him at the pool. *And now this?*

I'd had enough of this bullshit. It was the last fucking straw.

If Oliver wanted her, he could have her. Dressed in my clothes, too.

"Sure. Help yourself," I said, shrugging.

Nothing matters any more.

Bianca came forward, her eyes gleaming when she saw the selection hanging there. "Oh, you have some nice pieces here. Maybe a bit big for me, but I'm sure I'll find something that will make your brother happy."

My stomach churned and I felt sick. Did she really have to rub it in that she was skinnier than me on top of everything else?

"He's not my brother," I said, rolling my eyes. The anger that had been simmering all day since she arrived was reaching boiling point. I was about to lose my shit and it wasn't going to be pretty.

"Hmmm . . . this black one will look sexy on me. Can I try it on?"

"Knock yourself out," I said, getting up from the bed and making my way to the door. I wasn't going to stand there and watch the bitch parade around in my clothes.

As I headed for the door, I looked back and saw her slip out of her dress. No underwear. *Figures.*

Slamming into a hard chest once again, I sucked in a breath as Oliver's hands gripped my upper arms.

"Where are you going?" The smirk he greeted me with was more than I could handle.

"As far away from here as I can," I said, bile swirling in my gut. I was going to throw up if he didn't get out of my way. He made me sick.

Fuck this party. I never wanted it anyway.

And fuck Bianca, and Oliver too.

"Don't be ridiculous. You can't do that."

"Watch me."

"Ollie, come help me choose," Bianca's grating voice chimed back in. "Your sister has an amazing wardrobe. I wish I'd known years ago."

"At least one of us has good taste," I said dryly. I watched Oliver's face turn stone cold.

It went right over Bianca's head. She frowned and stared at me, a perplexed expression on her face. "Come to think of it, I've never seen you wear any of this stuff. You're always dressed in shorts or jeans. This is wasted on you."

"*Ollie?*" I sneered, pushing past him.

I flew down the stairs and didn't look back. It was time I stopped making a complete and utter fool of myself. I had to get my shit together where Oliver was concerned. Damn, I'd turned eighteen today and yet he still had the power to make me feel like that twelve-year-old child in the car on the way home from the airport.

Unwanted.

An irritation.

Not good enough for him.

"Maya, wait," he called after me. For a split second I wanted to stop dead in my tracks to hear what he wanted. No. Get out. Get away.

All Oliver King wanted was to humiliate me further.

I got it now. He was pretending to be nice to me earlier so that he could put me in my place once Bianca arrived. They'd laugh and make fun of me—of how naive I was.

Bianca's giggles drifted toward me. Yeah, I didn't need any more confirmation than that. As I reached the bottom of the stairs I saw Quinn, all dressed up and looking gorgeous.

"Bee?"

"Get me the fuck out of here. Please."

That's the great thing about having a bff. No further words were necessary. She grabbed her purse and hooked into my arm, pulling me toward the door.

"Where to?"

"Anywhere but here." I blinked fast, feeling the burn in my throat.

The car door clicked open.

"Sure. Hop in. I know just the place."

"You don't mind missing the party?" I said, swallowing hard.

"Of course not, silly. If you aren't there, there isn't much point is there?"

She started the engine and pulled off. With every mile we drove away, the weight on my shoulders lightened.

"Where are you taking me?"

She laughed. "Where every girl should be on her eighteenth birthday."

I left it at that, not really caring where we went. She had sensed that I didn't want to talk and for once in her life, she hadn't thrown a thousand questions my way. I'd sat huddled into the corner, my arms folded and my lips pursed tightly together.

Quinn knew me well enough to know that she wouldn't get a word out of me in my current state. She'd wait till I was ready and then the dam walls would burst.

I didn't really have to say anything either. She'd glanced at me and said one word. "Oliver?"

I'd nodded. That was all it took for her to know my state of mind. We drove without talking, but she cranked the music up so loud that chatting was impossible. It was her way of showing me that she understood and would wait until I was ready to let it all out.

Fifteen minutes later, she parked the car.

"A strip club? Are you fucking crazy? We'll never get in."

"Not unless we know the right people—which I just so happen to. We are getting laid tonight. You, missy, are going to have the time of your life. Fuck Oliver King. And, F.Y.I., there are some delicious hunks in there."

"Are you serious?" I breathed, gaping at Quinn.

She smiled reassuringly at me. "Never been more so. Oliver has fucked with your mind long enough. It's time to let that shit go. You're damn legal now, so let's do this!"

At the entrance, she flashed a card at the security slash bouncer dude. He let us in, no questions asked. "Damn, I'm impressed," I said, meaning every word.

My eyes widened as I drank it all in. I'd never been to a place like this. It wasn't a sleazy strip club at all. Loud music pierced my eardrums and there were bodies gyrating on a large dance floor.

"Let's get a drink first," she said as she headed for the bar. Shit, I was eighteen, not twenty-one. How would we pull this off?

"Two spritzers," she said, sliding money across the bar.

"Sure," the barman said, winking at Quinn.

Oh boy. Trouble was brewing and I was just going along for the ride.

Quinn was right. Fuck Oliver King.

Chapter 17
MAYA

EVENING

Minutes later we were sipping on tall, refreshing drinks containing large doses of alcohol. This shit was illegal, but I wasn't complaining. It was my birthday and I could get drunk if I wanted to. In fact, I was hell bent on it—the first few sips alone had helped me relax and made my head spin ever so slightly. *More of that stuff and I'll be spinning like a ballerina on crack.*

We watched a group of people leave a booth and headed straight for it. I needed to sit down; my knees were shaking that much.

"Hey Quinn, about time you came to the club. I'm glad to see you used your special card." The owner of the sexy voice was tall and built, his hard muscles on display through his tight, black, sleeveless t-shirt. His biceps flexed as he held onto the backrest of the seat and leaned over to kiss Quinn on the forehead, keeping his eyes glued to my breasts the entire time.

"Hey, Jason. I brought my best friend. It's her first time at a club and she needs some initiating. Maya just turned eighteen today."

Quinn knew hot men like Jason and never told me? She had some explaining to do.

The way Jason grinned at me, I thought he was going to eat me alive. Lust sparked in his eyes as his gaze raked up and down my body. Since I hadn't dressed up for the party before leaving the house, I was still dressed in what Larissa called my "slutty attire" of shorts and a loose top—braless, of course. I hated wearing underwear most of the time, so when I hung out in my bedroom, I stayed away from those restrictive garments.

"I like what I see. Happy birthday, Maya." His hand went to his crotch and he cupped his package unashamedly. "I have a birthday gift for you, darling."

Unsure of how to react to such blatant sexuality, I tried to hide my blush behind my glass as I giggled nervously and took a huge sip of my drink for more courage. This shit better work faster. I needed to get over my fucking shyness where guys were concerned.

Jason slid into the seat beside me with his eyes pinned on my boobs. Why did men always go there?

His gaze finally drifted back to my eyes. "Darling, where have you been hiding all my life? Quinn never told me she had a friend as beautiful as you." He took hold of my hand and placed it on his erection. "Not many girls do this to my cock any more. You're special, beautiful."

Quinn had a worried expression on her face. "Slow down, Jason. Jesus, Maya's not your dinner, you know," she scolded.

A slow grin spread over Jason's face. "I've just regained my appetite, Quinn, and I'm mighty hungry. Need to eat soon. And I know what I want for dinner . . . and dessert."

I sucked in a breath. Holy hell, he was direct. He was scaring and turning me on at the same time. But why the fuck is Oliver still in my mind? I could practically picture the scorn on his face if he saw me. Good. If this would make Oliver mad, I was all for it.

Drawing on all the false courage the alcohol had given me, I squeezed his cock through the denim. It was hard as granite and throbbed in my hand.

"Babe, you're something else, you know," Jason breathed on my neck, his breath warm and heavy.

"So I've been told," I said, smiling at how easy this was turning out to be. I'd never thought I'd be able to pull something like this off, but here I was holding a stranger's dick in my hand minutes after meeting him. What did that say about me? Fuck, I really didn't care. Quinn was right; I had to let go. Jason was clearly experienced and he wanted me—that much was clear.

Unlike someone else who rejected me. Shunned and snubbed me at every turn.

Quinn coughed, drawing our attention back to her. "Um, I've just spotted an old friend at the bar. Behave you two. Or actually—don't. Have fun."

My heart beat in my ears. With Quinn there, I knew Jason would be more talk than action, but now she was gone.

"So Maya, how does it feel to be eighteen? I've forgotten," Jason said, his hand on the top of my thigh.

"Um . . . how old are you?" Panic rose in my chest as my gaze narrowed in on the fine lines on the sides of his face. If he found out how little experience I had, he'd probably lose all interest. *More fucking rejection.*

"Ten years older than you, babe. But don't panic, I'll be gentle. I like my chicks young and a little inexperienced. Makes it so much more exciting to teach you. Worn-out whores bore me."

Well, at least he was honest. That was more than I could say for most men. I knew exactly where I stood with Jason. He wanted to fuck me and he wasn't afraid to admit it.

Why the fuck not? I could think of worse things than spending a night of pleasure with Jason. I liked that he was experienced and could guide me.

Jason's hand slid around my neck and pulled me closer to him. The warmness of his hand, the self-assured possessiveness, the desire in his eyes—it all felt good. His mouth covered mine as he tasted my lips.

"Jesus, darling, if your pussy tastes anything like your mouth, I'm in fucking trouble, you know?"

He made me feel good. Wanted. Desired.

Just what I needed.

His hand moved over my ribs and under my top, finding my breast and squeezing.

"Fuck, I love a woman who has the confidence to not wear a bra. You're making me wild, babe." His voice was deep and husky at my ear as he rolled a hard nipple between his fingers, pulling just enough to send pure pleasure shooting straight to my core. I threw back my head, exposing my neck to him, moaning softly.

"Fuck me. What the fuck?"

I could swear the booming voice sounded like Oliver's.

"Get away from her, asshole."

The warmth of Jason's hand and breath left me. What happened? My eyes flew open and were met with dark brown, angry eyes.

"What the fuck, Maya?" Oliver glared at me, his jaw tight, disgust and anger on his face. He'd pulled Jason off me—my new friend hung by his shirt collar, bewildered by what had just happened.

"Hey, let go, dude. Who the fuck do you think you are to interrupt?"

"I'm your worst fucking nightmare if you don't disappear in three seconds, dude," Oliver spat out.

"I saw her first, asshole." Jason punched Oliver in the stomach with his elbow. I couldn't help liking Jason just a little bit more right then. At least he had the damn guts to want to fight for me. Not that he'd win against Oliver, but it was sweet anyway.

Out of breath from the punch, Oliver narrowed his eyes at me. "Maya, get the fuck in my car now if you don't want me to smash pretty boy's face. I'm two seconds away from rearranging it."

Oliver meant it, of that I was certain. He had a thing for punching guys.

"How . . . how did you find me? And what are you doing here? The party—"

"I followed you and Quinn. Except I couldn't find fucking parking. Had to leave my car two blocks away. You're lucky I got here when I did."

"Or what, Oliver?" I cocked my head and waited for his answer.

"Babe, who the fuck is this dude?" Jason asked as he took a step closer to me.

Oliver growled, his fists clenched into balls, his knuckles white. "You're still here, asshole? Don't make me hurt you."

I sighed. "It's okay, Jason, he's my stepbrother."

"Back off, dude, I'm not going to hurt her," Jason said to Oliver. "Your sister is okay with me."

I watched Jason stagger backwards as Oliver punched him once on the jaw, followed up with a jab in the pit of his stomach. Before I could say anything, Oliver had reached out and grabbed my upper arm, dragging me across the seat.

"You are coming home with me. I don't want to hear another fucking word."

Roughly, he dragged me by the arm, pulling me toward the door.

"Quinn—"

"Fuck Quinn. Jason can tell her what happened."

"You're hurting me."

He laughed. "You think this is pain? You have no fucking idea, little bee."

Chapter 18
OLIVER

EVENING

This was getting fucking old. How many more times would I have to pull guys off Maya? My stomach churned when I thought of what I saw in that booth. Little slut was about to give it up to fucking Jason.

I knew Jason. He was a real ladies man. Woman loved him and he usually had his pick at every party I'd seen him at. Yet, I couldn't blame him for wanting her. There was something about Maya that just made men's dicks howl for her pussy. And I could hardly bear watching it any longer.

She tried to pull away from me, but my grip just tightened around her arm, practically dragging her along with me. If I needed to, I'd throw the little bitch over my shoulder and carry her to my car.

As for Quinn—she was in for a lashing of my tongue when I saw her again. What the fuck was she trying to do? I could strangle her. One minute Maya was getting ready for her party, the next she'd disappeared. If Larissa hadn't witnessed it all and told me what happened I would've wasted time looking for her around the pool or in the library, and then there was no way I would have found her in time.

"Is there no fucking end to your slutty ways?" I barked. "Why would you go to a club dressed like that? It's asking for trouble."

Marching through the street with long strides, Maya struggled to keep up with my pace. I didn't care. I just wanted to get out of there and forget what I saw.

A few minutes later, I shoved her into the car and slammed the door shut, locking it in case she tried to escape while I rounded the car. By the time I got in on my side, she'd folded her arms across her chest and was staring straight ahead of her. The way she lifted her chin already made my balls ache.

"Start wearing underwear, Maya. Don't let me catch you without it again."

Maya was trouble.

A dirty slut and more trouble than I needed in my life. The sweet side I'd seen that morning—the side that pulled at my heart—was just a show. I bet she used it to get guys hot for her. Yet I couldn't let it go. I'd watched, mesmerized for a full minute or two as the prick made his moves on her, strangely turned on. The raging fire that burned through me was difficult to ignore. When his hand slipped under her top, I totally lost my shit. Why was it that every guy in the universe could cop a feel but I couldn't touch her?

She sat there quietly, not moving. Fuck. Quiet Maya wasn't something I knew how to deal with. Raging and calling me names, yeah. That I could handle. Sweet and soft Maya, I liked in spite of myself. But quiet?

"Why, Oliver? Why do you always show up at the worst fucking time? I don't get it. It's not like I storm in on you and Bianca even when your damn headboard slams against my wall."

"It's different." I mumbled. Fuck, I couldn't even explain it to myself. How would I make Maya understand that seeing another male touch her made me insane—without actually sounding crazy.

"Different? How?"

"I don't know. All I do know is that you're one of the biggest sluts I've come across. And that's saying a lot."

Her lips pursed together and I thought she'd slap me—her eyes were that murderous.

"What's it to you if I'm a slut? Who I kiss, who I make out with, and who I fuck has nothing to do with you."

I sighed. My fucking head was hurting and I just wanted to take her home where I knew she'd be under the same roof as me.

She looked at me from under her lashes. "Where's Bianca?"

"I sent her back to LA. She didn't look good in any of your dresses." That was a lie—I forbade Bianca to even try one on. Asking her to come to Santa Barbara was a huge mistake. I was already bored with her and her clingy ways the minute she'd arrived, so sending her packing was one of the easiest decisions of the night.

As we pulled into the driveway, Maya sucked in a breath when she saw that all the cars had left. "Where's everyone?"

"You need to ask? Of course everyone left after you did. No point in having a fucking party if you weren't there. Larissa cried and Alec was white as a ghost. I told your father I was going after you and that he should ask everyone to leave."

Maya dropped her head, tears flowing down her cheeks. "Oh my God, I keep fucking things up for other people, don't I? I . . . I'm sorry," she choked out.

I didn't know what to say to that. Her hurt and pain were so raw and evident that it took me completely by surprise. I'd only really ever seen the feisty side, never her vulnerability before that day.

I wanted to pull her into a hug and kiss her cheeks. I wanted to tell her that I was sorry, too. I wanted to make it all better for her.

Only I couldn't.

I couldn't let her know how torn she made me feel. How I panicked when I didn't know where she was.

How Bianca meant nothing to me.

How I was relieved and pissed off at the same time when I found her.

How seeing another man's paws on her twisted my gut.

Chapter 19
MAYA

LATE EVENING

Oliver must've taken pity on me because he let me slip back into the house without having to face Daddy or Larissa.

"Go up to your room. Take a shower and go to bed. I'll tell our parents that you're safe and I've brought you back." His voice was stern, and I decided not to argue.

During the whole ride home, I'd felt dirty and disgusted with myself. I couldn't blame Oliver for thinking what he did about me. Yet there wasn't any point in trying to convince him otherwise.

I ran the shower, feeling completely drained and beyond exhausted. Stripping off, I got under the streaming water, letting it wash away all the dirt that clung to me.

A pang speared my heart. What would Mom say if she saw me now? She'd be disappointed in the woman I'd become. Shame washed over me and I hung my head, sobbing for my mother, missing her so damn much that my heart squeezed in my chest.

I'd fucked up in so many ways. *It all is just too much.*

My skin wrinkling from standing under the water for so long, I turned the taps off and dried myself quickly. My eyes fell on my blades. I hadn't cut in a long while.

After Oliver left when I was sixteen, I'd used blades for the first time. I never cut deep, only making faint marks on my skin. It was more the idea of just holding them between my fingers and trying to imagine what went through my mother's head when she did it.

I was way too much of a coward to actually make myself bleed. Whenever I'd accidentally cut myself, or if anyone else was bleeding, I just about fainted. There was no way in hell I could do a job like Daddy who cut and sliced people for a living. No way I wanted to follow in his footsteps—although he tried to convince me on several occasions that I had the capability to become a surgeon.

Slipping on the new Victoria's Secret underwear that had been untouched in my drawer for over a year, I started methodically combing through my wet hair.

"It's all too much," I whispered to the image in the mirror. Looking at my reflection was the closest I could ever get to Mom.

I put down the comb and picked up the blades.

I closed my eyes and let go.

Of the hurt in my heart.

Of the fear in my gut.

Of desolation.

The overwhelming emptiness.

I was tired of feeling that all the time.

My whole life flashed before my eyes.

It had to stop.

Present

Chapter 20
MAYA

"Let me help you. Don't be so fucking stubborn." Oliver's arm slid around my waist and he lifted me up off the ground and bundled me into the passenger seat of his SUV. He reached over to fasten the seatbelt, pressing his arm against my chest.

"I'm not a kid, Oliver," I said, still annoyed that he treated me like a child after all these years. I was over it.

Both my arms rested on my lap as I stared at him. We'd come up with a story to tell my father about where I'd been the last few days. I worried that he'd be suspicious when the stepbrother I never had any real form of relationship with suddenly was the one bringing me home.

"Then stop acting like a kid. And stop worrying about your old man. He's not going to know anything about what happened—unless you don't keep your side of the bargain, of course." The smirk on Oliver's face was the one I knew so well. It was also the expression that drove me crazy—sexy in a wicked way; it twisted my stomach.

"I never agreed to be your fucking sex slave. My answer is no. Find yourself another of those bimbos you used to bring home and fuck all night long when you were in college. The one's who'd scream your name while your fucking headboard slammed against my wall keeping me awake."

"I bet you were enjoying it. Wishing it was you I was eating out. I bet you had your hands down your pants."

I cut him off before he could taunt me further. "You'd lose a lot of money if you bet on that. I'd either put my headphones on and drown the noise out or I'd—" I clamped a hand over my mouth, realizing I'd just said too much.

Oliver growled in my ear. "Or *what*, Maya? What would you do while I was fucking a girl with only a wall separating us?"

"I'd climb through the window, smart ass, and leave the house so I didn't have to be subjected to your evil plans. I know you did it to get to me."

"Don't flatter yourself, darling. A man has needs that must be taken care of." He grabbed hold of my chin and squeezed, forcing my face up to meet his gaze. His lips drew into a thin line. "Where did you go, Maya, if you weren't in your bed like a good little girl?"

"That's none of your damn business, darling stepbrother," I said, sneering. "The point is that I wasn't there to listen to you and your bitches fucking one another to death."

"Maya, don't test me. I'm not asking again. Where the fuck did you go?" His eyes blazed as he pinned me with his gaze, biting down and clenching his jaw. He squeezed my cheeks so hard that my eyes watered.

"Let go of me. You're hurting me, asshole."

"You are going to suck my dick for every time you've ever called me a bad name. I'm turning you into my slut from this day forward. And I won't be easy on you. You thought I was fucking those chicks hard? Baby, you have no fucking idea what I'm going to do to you."

"Touch me and . . . and—"

"Yeah . . . and what? You'll tell Daddy? Not if I tell him first." A vein ticked in his jaw as he reached into his pocket and pulled out his phone.

My eyes widened. "You're going to call him now?"

He laughed—a deep laugh from his stomach. "No, that won't be necessary after you see these pictures on my phone. All I need to do is press the send button to tell the old man the story." He opened a window on his phone and held it out to me. "Look."

He scrolled through picture after picture—it was all there. Pictures of when he found me in the bathroom, the cuts on my wrists, the bandages still wrapped around them. I sucked in a breath, feeling sick to my stomach. I wanted to pass out or throw up or both. I closed my eyes to block out the images. This would crush my father. It would bring the big man to his knees if I died in the same manner my mother had. Trembling, I rubbed my fist against my chest to ease the pain in my heart.

"It's all a mistake. I never meant to go so deep—it won't happen again. Please don't tell Daddy." I slouched forward in the seat, ready to do anything to prevent this going any further. Anything except have sex with my evil stepbrother. I just couldn't do it. The man undid me in ways I didn't understand; having sex with him would be fatal for me.

His voice was gruff. "You're begging. Good, I like that."

"Yes, I'm begging. Please don't make me have sex with you. Please. Please don't fuck me." My chin rested on my chest. Suddenly I was tired to the bone, all my energy drained. I just wanted to curl up and go to sleep for a hundred years.

"I'm sorry, but that's not going to cut it. For years I've been taunted by your tight little body. You've teased me with your skimpy outfits, flirted with my friends in front of me, fucking touched yourself while I watched—

driving me *insane* because I couldn't touch you." The harsh tone in his voice cut through me, bitterness lying just beneath the surface. "You belong to me and there's nothing you can do about it. I saved your wretched life—it fucking belongs to me. You're mine to do with as I please, little bee. Get used to it. I'm never letting you go."

Stunned by his words, my head jerked up. He meant every single word. I was totally fucked and I knew it. Oliver always managed to get what he wanted, and now he wanted me.

Why? I didn't know.

A plaything for his perverted pleasure? There were so many women willing to fall into his bed; he had no problem getting whomever he wanted. And he always had Bianca. She was already his plaything, eager and willing. God, that damn headboard had reminded me enough times of how he fucked her.

To get me back for something I'd done to him? Nothing could ever have been that bad. For fuck sake, I was only a kid most of the time. He'd said so enough times himself.

"Why, Oliver? It's so *wrong*."

He stared down at me in silence for a long moment. My heartbeat sped up in the hope he'd reconsider his demand. Surely he'd realize this couldn't go anywhere. He'd use me, abuse me, break my heart and throw me aside when he was done. I couldn't allow it. I had to fight—for my own protection if nothing else.

"*Because I can*. All these years I've watched you act like a slut around other boys. I watched them kiss you. Touch you. I watched you put your lips around another man's dick. But now—now it's my turn and you're my slut. Your life belongs to me." The tips of his fingers brushed over my lips. "Hell, all of you belongs to me—these lips," the back of his hand traced down my neck to my chest. He cupped a breast in his palm and squeezed. "These tits." His hand slid downward over my ribs. "This pussy, your ass. Mine." His hand slid between my thighs, cupping my mound. It felt warm, even as it sent a cold shiver up my spine. He rubbed his fingers against my pussy, the friction driving me crazy. I wanted to scream; instead I clamped my legs together.

His tone softened. "Don't fight it, little bee. It's going to happen—just go with it; accept it. There is no escape."

His mouth came crashing down on mine, bruising my lips as he stole the breath from my lungs.

Chapter 21
MAYA

We drove home in silence. My mind scrambled around frantically, trying to come up with a way out of this dilemma. There had to be something I could do or say that would make my stepbrother change his mind.

Peering at his face with a sideways glance, I stiffened. Oliver's jaw was set, his expression hard and unrelenting. I'd need a fucking miracle to get out of this.

"I have a boyfriend, you know. He won't be okay with this." My comment was met with stony silence; for some reason it frightened me more than if he ranted and raved. In my peripheral vision I could see him purse his lips even tighter. "Even Daddy approves of him," I offered, as if I was trying to convince him that Gerard was real.

Both hands tightened around the steering wheel as if he was trying to strangle it. I was pretty sure he was picturing me. Or maybe Gerard? I didn't peg Oliver for a jealous man. His reputation as a ladies' man still hung around college, even though he'd left several years ago. I'd heard he often shared his women with his friends, so I assumed he didn't have issues with screwing around.

"That ends now. Text him. Tell him it's over." His voice was gruff and demanding.

Crossing my arms, I snorted. I seriously didn't care if it was unladylike. "Are you fucking crazy? I happen to like him. It's not always about you, Oliver King."

He turned his head and gave me a smile that knocked my breath away. "Oh yeah, it is. It's all about me, baby. You're going to find that out soon enough." His hand went to his crotch, cupping his package.

I rolled my eyes. What was it with men and their balls? "You're obsessed with your own dick. And no, I'm not going to break up with my boyfriend." I paused for dramatic effect—and to give it time to sink into his think skull. "Certainly not because you told me to and never via text. That's just rude."

"Oh, and slitting your wrists and bleeding out on the bathroom floor isn't?"

His words stung. I should have known he'd have some smart ass comeback. He always did. I leaned over and punched him in the arm. The impact made my wrist ache, but punching him gave me a weird satisfaction. "I hate you," I said, rubbing my wrist.

He chuckled softly. "I bet you do. That still doesn't change anything. I'm looking forward to first, punishing you, and second, teaching you. And the best part? You'll beg me for more."

Never was there a man more conceited than my stepbrother. He needed taking down a notch or two. "Oliver King, if you were the last man on the face of the earth, I wouldn't want to fuck you." I pulled up my nose in disgust. "You think banging a woman so hard she screams is the only way to fuck. You have no idea. Not every woman wants to be treated like a whore. Until you act like a man—a real man—I doubt there is much you can teach me. So quit this little game you're playing because I'm really not interested."

I turned in my seat and stared out of the window. I'd cried way too many tears over my stepbrother through the years and I was done with that. "I never asked you to save me." My voice had a bitter edge to it that I couldn't conceal. "All I want from you is to be left the fuck alone. Stay away from me—you've been damn good at it in the past, so I don't really understand what's changed now."

The SUV pulled up into the driveway. I clicked my seatbelt and pushed the door open, jumping out the second the vehicle came to a stop. I nearly stumbled and fell, but I managed to right myself and storm up to the house as fast as I could, running from the man who could ruin me with his demands and break me with his words. I cursed the day my stepbrother came into my life. Nothing had been the same since.

I rang the doorbell, hoping to God that Miriam, the housekeeper, would open the door and not Daddy or my bitch of a stepmother. I glanced back while waiting for the door to open. Of course I didn't have my key or purse with me. One does not plan for an emergency hospital visit, and all Oliver had brought me was a long sleeve shirt to pull over my wrists to hide the bandages.

Oliver appeared behind me, his warm breath on my neck.

"Nobody's home. It's Saturday and they're away for the weekend. Miriam has the weekend off. I promised our parents I'd look after you when you got back, so I guess I have to stick to that."

I turned on my heels and faced him, leaning back against the front door. I lifted my chin and met his gaze. "Just tell me why? Why are you so damn intent on torturing me? I thought eventually you'd get over it and move on. Surely you have better things to do than waste your time on me?"

My words must've shocked him, because his eyes widened and his mouth hung slightly open. For the second time since I'd know him, he didn't look at me with contempt. He leaned forward and placed a hand on each side of my head, caging me in. He stared at me for a long moment, his eyes searching my face.

"You don't get it do you? I've waited years for this moment."

I sucked in a breath. "What do you mean?"

"Since that day at the pool, I've felt the pull you have on me. You draw me to you like a fucking magnet."

"I . . . I do?"

He placed a finger under my chin and lifted my face to his. "I've waited all this fucking time for you to grow up. I've held off—been a fucking saint when all I've wanted to do was to claim you."

"What?"

"You heard me. I've been fucking obsessed with you since the day you grew a pair of tits. I want you. I crave you. And now, finally, I *own* you."

Chapter 22
MAYA

It was just the two of us, Daddy and me, since I was a baby. I'd never really known a mother—mine had committed suicide when I was eleven months old. Daddy told me it was "the baby blues" that took her to heaven. At the time I didn't know what exactly that was, but it didn't sound too bad if it had anything to do with music. I loved music, and Daddy always listened to blues, so I presumed he was thinking about her when he listened to it with that faraway look in his eyes.

Imagine my shock when I discovered she'd slit her wrists because she couldn't handle having me. *I'm the reason she couldn't cope.* I'd caused her to take her own life to escape me. I'd read all about it on Google. Quinn had helped research it.

As I grew up, I became morbidly fascinated with suicide and cutting. I wanted to know firsthand what my mother's pain felt like. *Experience* her suffering and anguish. Maybe it would make me feel closer to her if I understood what she went through.

I never got it, though. Megan Childs stayed as much a mystery to me as ever.

My flesh hurt, sometimes it bled, but I never felt close enough to her. Each time I tried to make some sort of connection with her I'd cut just a little deeper in the hopes of sensing her agony. After all, if it weren't for me, she'd still be alive.

And Daddy? Even though he had Larissa, I still caught him with the same forlorn expression in his eyes when he thought nobody noticed. *I* did, because I'd known it so well for as far back as I could remember.

"Princess Maya, you're growing up too fast. Every year on your birthday, it's as if you look more and more like your mother . . . it's spooky." Hurt radiated from the gentle man's eyes as he rubbed at the ache in his chest. If only I could take his pain away. *Change the way I look.* I was causing the only person I loved on the face of the earth more distress than he could bear.

I'd always been Daddy's "Princess Maya." But then it changed on my thirteenth birthday and he stopped looking at me. He seemed relieved when I said I was staying at a friend's house. And he hadn't called me Princess Maya in a long time before my birthday—not since he met and married Larissa, the bitch who thought she could take my mother's place in my father's heart.

Knowing that I looked so much like the woman who caused my father so much pain, I hated looking into a mirror. Unlike Larissa—that woman was freaking obsessed with her looks. She spent a fortune on new clothes, hair, treatments, whatever she thought would make her look young and pretty.

Yet here I am, staring into the goddamn mirror. What the fuck happened to me?

First, I'd been channeling a dead woman's pain to no avail.

Then Oliver happened. Before he left, I'd only ever thought about it as a way to feel closer to my mom. After he'd left, I needed it to take my pain away. I thought trying to get closer to my mom would help. It was the tipping point—the last thing that stood between me and the blades slicing through my skin, driving me to harm my own body.

And now?

I'd become an object of . . . payback. Someone else's way to escape their pain. I had no illusions about Oliver's motives—he was as damaged as I was, and he was merely trying to find ways to escape his own agony. *But why does it have to be me he's picking on?* Was I such an easy target? I never thought of myself as weak, not until Oliver crashed my life. Something about him just got to me. Every time.

My brain scrambled to work it all out. Flashbacks from things I hadn't understood before rushed through the jumbled mess that was my mind. I remembered a conversation that hadn't made any sense at the time. I'd overheard our parents talking just after they got married, Larissa pleading with Daddy.

"Please, Alec, give the boy a chance. It's because of his own demons that Oliver is acting up. Once he grows up and understands it better, he'll outgrow it," she'd said in her sugar sweet voice.

"Larissa, he's a wild card. He's sixteen, on the edge between being a boy and man. Oliver needs to accept what happened." My father's voice was grim. "And he better stay away from Maya. If he hurts one hair on her head, God knows what I'll do."

"Don't be ridiculous, Alec. Why would Oliver even look at Maya? For God's sake, she's his little stepsister. He's had a girlfriend already. You have nothing to worry about."

That was all I could hear from their conversation before I had to move away from the door. I didn't understand half of it because I'd only just met Oliver.

I was still trying to put all the pieces together, figure out why Oliver would be as obsessed with me as he said he was. It didn't make sense. He had access to as much pussy as he wanted. His face, his body, his cock—everything was perfect. It was only his eyes that gave him away. Angry. Determined. Set on revenge for a wrong done to him. And I was the one who was going to pay the price.

He was as fucked up as ever.

He'd come for me—like I always knew he would. I wanted to scream.

For the first time in a very long time, I really looked at myself. At what I'd become. On the outside I looked like Snow White—my favorite childhood fairy tale and the one I used to insist Daddy read to me just about every night before I went to sleep.

The similarities between us were uncanny: I had the same long black hair and the palest of skin if I didn't get out into the sun for a tan. My full lips were stained red, and I even had the evil stepmother who wanted me dead. But it was so very obvious that Prince Charming was nowhere to be found.

Instead I'd been delivered into the hands of a monster. An ogre who wanted to devour my fucking soul.

And the fucked-up thing about it all? I wanted him too. Because I, Maya Christina Childs, craved to be owned by my depraved step brother. I wanted him. Needed *him* to take *my* pain away. Because if anyone could erase my constant sorrow, it would be Oliver King.

I didn't understand it; I simply knew it to be true. How? *I don't know.*

All I did know was this—I needed him like I needed air.

We were using one another to fix our damaged souls.

Jolted from my thoughts, I jumped when Oliver's arm slid around my waist and pulled me back against his chest. Like a ragdoll, I went limp. There was no point in fighting this. I'd known it was coming since the first time he looked at me with that scowl between his brows and lust burned in his eyes. It was still there, and had only grown more severe.

Everything about this man was intense. Dark. Forbidden.

It only made me want him more.

Crave his touch on my skin.

His lips on mine.

Him buried deep inside me.

Maybe then I'd know what it felt like to belong. To be owned. Completely.

My mind fought it. Struggled for control. Told me what I wanted was so wrong. Yet every cell in my body screamed for him. I was finally going to belong to someone again.

Our gazes met in the mirror. His face was deadpan and unreadable. But in his eyes burned desire like I'd never seen before.

Dropping my head back to rest on his broad chest, his hand gripped my throat and squeezed, marking his possession. Words weren't necessary. We both wanted this. Craved it for redemption from our damaged souls and shattered hearts.

He breathed heavily. "Maya. Finally." Oliver's chest heaved and warm breath dispersed across my skin, scattering goose bumps over the entire surface.

The moment I'd waited for all my life had arrived. The moment I'd belong to someone who wanted me as much as I wanted him. Because in spite of all the fucked-upness of what was happening, there was no doubt in my mind that we truly wanted one another, no matter how unclear or impure the reasons. Eyes wide open, I wanted to soak every minuscule detail in—I wanted to remember this moment forever.

The air in the room sucked out leaving a vacuum—it was just us.

Tainted. Deviant. Beyond saving.

Chapter 23
MAYA

"Oliver, this is so wrong." The despair in my voice was palpable. I was torn in two between my need for this man and what I thought was right. Or let me rephrase: what I *knew* was wrong.

As far as I knew, Oliver King had his shit together and a shiny future ahead of him in the IT industry. Several years ago I'd learned that he was, in fact, a genius sought after by major corporations. Yet he was far from being nerdy; my stepbrother could pass for a male model any day. He had the face and the body for it, not to mention the cocky attitude. By comparison, I was a fucking mess. My very identity hung by a thread.

"I've wanted you for all this time. Nothing is going to stop me any longer." He tilted his chin up slightly as if he was waiting for me to challenge him. "You owe me your life. I'm simply taking what is rightfully mine. There is nothing wrong with that."

Buttons scattered over the bathroom tile as he ripped the front of my shirt open, exposing my swollen breasts. He gripped a fist full of my hair and pushed my face forward, closer to the mirror. "Look at your face, little bee. So fucking beautiful. I don't think you have any idea just how gorgeous you are." My gaze shifted to my face. "It's mine. Those eyes that punish me, those lips that taunt me. Mine."

All I saw when I looked into the eyes reflecting back at me was my own arousal. Pupils dilated, eyelids heavy with lust. My lips full and dewy. Sweat breaking out over my skin from desire. I bit into my bottom lip, desperate to stop it from quivering.

The back of his hand caressed my skin—down my jawline, across my throat, lingering where my breasts were spilling over the cups of my bra. Mesmerized I watched in the mirror as his fingers stroked over the fabric, his thumb circling my nipple until it was on fire.

"Mine. These fucking tits are mine. Yet you let other boys touch them, suck them. I could kill you for that alone." He pinched the nipple between his fingers, twisting until I cried out. *Oh God*!

Both hands slid down my ribs to my hips, his thumbs pushing into the small of my back, pressing into my skin. "Undo the zipper," he commanded. Though his voice sounded calm and even, there was a definite undertone of power.

With shaky hands, I pulled the zipper down. The skirt fell away from my hips, dropping to the floor. "So fucking beautiful," he murmured, his calloused hands skimming over my hips, pushing my panties down, exposing my pale skin inch by inch. He bent down and removed the skirt and panties, sniffing my skin as he slowly straightened up again. "You smell so fucking good. I just want to eat you."

My thighs clenched together. God, I was sure my pussy was dripping. Every word from his filthy mouth was making me wetter and wetter. His hand caressed over my pussy. "So soft. So smooth. Just the way I love it. Mine. *My pussy*."

He pulled my head back, gripping my hair hard until my eyes watered from the pain. His lips were on my ear, hot, panting, delicious. "No other man will touch you again. You are mine and only mine. If you want to be a slut, you can be my slut. Are we clear on that?"

His half-crazed gaze met mine in the mirror as he waited for my answer. My throat burned and my chest heaved with pent-up emotion. I swallowed hard.

"Say it. Say you're mine." Why was it so damn important to him? So he could use me and throw me away when he was done? Was that his ultimate plan of revenge?

I closed my eyes. I couldn't say it. I wasn't any man's slut—yet I wanted to be his. My head screamed that this was wrong. A bad mistake. Yet I craved this; I couldn't wait to find out what he'd do next.

"Little bee, I'm waiting for you to say it." His voice had an agitated edge to it.

I shook my head. "N . . . no. I'm not yours."

"Oh baby, those are not the words I want to hear." His mouth turned upside down as he pursed his lips. My heartbeat sped up, thumping in my chest.

His foot kicked my legs apart as he pinned me to his body, one hand on my pussy, his palm pressing down possessively, while his other hand encased my throat, controlling exactly how much air I could suck into my lungs. I watched—wide eyed, my head spinning from lack of oxygen—as his nimble fingers spread my pussy open, searching for my core.

I wanted to fight, rib him with my elbow, and scream for him to let me go. His grip was too tight. I gasped for air, my arms flailing by my sides.

"Be still, little bee. Fighting makes it worse. Just relax." His voice was soothing, as if he were calming a child. He was right, the more I fought, the stronger his hold on me had become, and the more it turned me on. I couldn't understand what was happening to me, why I both hated and loved what he was doing to me, his possession so overwhelming and all-consuming that I had to give in and succumb.

I softened against him and immediately the hold around my windpipe loosened. I sucked air into my lungs, greedy for more, feeling it burn as it rushed into my body.

"Clever girl. The moment you submit to me is the moment I give you more freedom. Surrender, Maya; give yourself to me."

A wicked grin spread over his face as his thumb found my hard nub.

"Just as I thought. You're dripping wet." Two fingers found their way inside as his thumb kept circling my clit. I ground my ass against his erection, desperate for more.

"Ahhh, sweet surrender. You please me, little bee."

An orgasm was building, heightening every sense in my body. I wanted this so badly in spite of how hard I was trying to resist. Conflict tore at my mind and my body until I finally relaxed against Oliver's hard torso, willing to yield to him, careful to keep my eyes wide open so that I could absorb everything. Once I'd accepted that this was happening, that I wanted it to happen, I didn't want to miss a second of this torturous pleasure.

He pulled his fingers out and lifted them to his nose, sniffing my scent like a primal animal. "Fuck, you're so ready for me, aren't you, little bee? You've wanted this for a long time."

I bit down on my lip—hard enough to taste blood—to stop the words from tumbling from my lips. I'd never admit anything to him. Never.

He spun me around and lifted me off the floor, placing me on the counter in front of him. Pushing my knees apart, he smiled. His eyes gleamed when he took in the sight of my sex, setting my body on fire. Warmth spread to my cheeks and I tried to look away, but I couldn't. A low, soft rumble erupted from his chest and a thousand butterflies were set free inside my stomach.

Oliver chuckled softly, fully aware of the effect he had on me as he knelt down and gripped my thighs before licking over my pussy with one long stroke.

"Oh God," I whimpered. My legs trembled and I twisted my fingers tightly into his hair to stop myself from screaming.

"I will make you scream, little bee," he said. I was going fucking insane; my pussy throbbed. I pulled his face closer, and at the same time spread my legs wider, pushing myself forward into his mouth, wanting him to devour me.

"Fuck," I screamed as he fucked me with his tongue. I couldn't take much more. Spiraling out of control, my orgasm ripped through my body. I'd never felt anything like it. Every part of my body and soul felt alive—as if currents of electricity had been pumped into me.

"Oliver, oh God," I panted as he removed his face, covered in my juice, and came in for a kiss. His mouth devoured mine. All I could taste was myself on him. It was sexy as fuck.

When exactly he'd freed his cock, I had no idea. "I already checked your drawers. I know you've been on the pill for a while."

He'd sniffed around my room? *Sneaky bastard.* Before I could admonish or stop him, he'd pushed inside, bare. He groaned loudly in my ear as he inched his cock into me. "So fucking tight, my little bee."

I squeezed my eyes shut, feeling every inch of his cock sliding into me; I gasped as he pushed all the way in.

"What the fuck?" he cried out in my ear, pulling out. We both stared at the blood on his cock. "You're . . . you're a virgin?" His voice was hoarse and his eyes were nearly bugging out of his head.

Biting my lip to hold back my tears, I nodded.

"Sweet Jesus, why didn't you tell me?" he roared. "I just assumed . . . all the boys that always flock around you like a bitch in heat . . . fuck. *Fuck.* Are you okay?"

The concern on his face was adorable. He looked as if someone had just slapped him, hard. "I didn't know, little bee. I'm so fucking sorry."

"Don't stop now. I want this. If anyone was going to have my virginity, I'm—" I stopped talking and pulled him closer. "Please just finish. Just do it."

His eyes were on fire. "Are you sure?"

"Yes, I'm your slut, remember? Fuck me, Oliver. Please."

"Fuck, little bee, you are fucking killing me here. You have no idea."

He lifted me off the counter and carried me to his bedroom as if I would break. Laying me gently on the bed, he crawled over me, his cock rock hard.

Quivering, I spread my legs and guided him to my entrance. He leaned forward and kissed me softly while he inched his cock into me slowly. Oh so very, very slowly, taking so much care not to hurt me that I thought I'd burst.

"Fuck me already," I whined, desperate for the friction of his hardness inside me. Tears spilt down my cheeks. For the first time in my entire life I felt as if I really and truly belonged to someone.

"Don't cry, Maya. Please."

"It's happy tears. Girls do tears when they're sad *and* happy."

"Well let me make you really happy then," he said as he moved inside me, increasing the rhythm and speed.

I belonged to Oliver. I would be whatever he wanted.

There was nothing I wanted more than to finally be his.

Even if that meant I was his slut. His whore. It didn't matter what he called me as long as he gave me what I needed. Him.

Chapter 24
OLIVER

I pulled out of her slowly, the blood on my sheets further proof that she belonged only to me. All those years of torture, of imagining other boys dipping their dicks into my little bee, had nearly driven me insane.

I'd tried to hold back, restrain my movements once I was inside her, but I wanted her so fucking desperately that I had to struggle to keep control. This wasn't what I imagined it would be. Anger flared up in my gut. This wasn't supposed to be her first time.

Yet nothing pleased me more than to know I was first. My heart nearly burst with joy—a feeling I'd forgotten ever existed.

This is so fucking twisted. I'm mad and happy at the same time. Maya was fucking with my head. That was nothing new.

It was just supposed to be sex—raw, carnal lust. Feeding my desires. I didn't want to care if I'd hurt her or have to control myself when I fucked her. In my mind it was always rough, dirty, exciting. Pleasure mixed with pain. No feelings, no fluffy shit—only ownership. I'd use her as revenge for all the wrongs done to me in this life.

My stomach twisted into a tight knot. *Fuck, instead of getting rid of my obsession she's pulled me in deeper.*

Now I'd had her, and there was no fucking way I could stop. I'd only ever want more. I wanted to tie her to my bed and fuck her until she couldn't walk. I wanted to hear her scream my name. I wanted every part of her.

Like a slap in the face, the realization pierced my mind: this was only the *beginning* of my obsession. How had I believed it would end once I'd been inside her? After what happened, there was no way in hell I'd ever let her go. Ever let another man touch her.

Something had shifted and it frightened the fuck out of me.

The worst part? I had absolutely no fucking control over it. None whatsoever. That was a first for Oliver King. I'd always thought that I was the one in control. Now I learned that it was the other way around; fear broke out on my skin; my mind was spinning.

Only I knew she could never really be mine. I was fucked—my DNA tainted. And I was taking her straight to hell with me.

Think, Oliver. Think.

I was getting both of us deeper into a mess of fucking epic proportions. Was I prepared to take the consequences? Was I even ready to? Before, fucking Maya was all in my head. Now shit had gotten real and I couldn't see any way out.

She reached out and cupped my cheek in her hand, smiling shyly before burying her face in my neck. I cradled the back of her head, holding her against me, feeling every inch of her soft curves against my hard body.

Fuck. Something inside me stirred and I didn't know what the fuck it was. It wasn't anything I could put my finger on. My analytical brain kept searching for answers, trying to make sense of this jumble in my mind. It scrambled in circles, confused and defunct. Unable to comprehend what the fuck was happening to me.

My heart was cracking open, little by fucking little, as she clawed her way inside the one place that was totally forbidden.

I'd take her body. I'd control her mind. But I wasn't going anywhere near her heart—or mine. Those were totally off-limits. It was just the way it had to be.

Rising from the bed, I fetched a wet washcloth, cleaning between her legs. She watched me with wide eyes as if she couldn't believe what had just happened. Her skin was flushed and she wouldn't meet my gaze, turning her eyes down every time I looked at her.

Leaving her alone for a moment so that she could compose herself—no, so I could compose myself—I went back to the bathroom and rinsed the washcloth, then wiped the remains of blood from my cock. I sucked in a breath when I realized it was the first time I'd taken a girl's virginity. Every other woman I'd ever fucked had been used before.

The significance wasn't lost on me. Although I hadn't known before I fucked her. Why hadn't she said something? Stopped me? Would I have listened? I was a monster in Maya's eyes, evil and twisted. She was right.

Exhausted from trying to figure this out, I went back to the bedroom.

She'd curled into a little ball on the bed, her arms hugging her knees. She looked so fucking vulnerable, so alone between the white sheets, her dark hair spread out like a fan around her head. An overwhelming urge to make it right, to make her feel better, flooded my heart.

Crawling back onto the bed, I spooned behind her back and pulled her into my body, caging her in with my arms. She stiffened for a second before relaxing into me. We fit so fucking perfectly together—how could this be wrong?

Two broken souls.

Damaged.

Searching to belong.

Finding one another in the most unexpected way.

"You okay?" I whispered against her skin, kissing her shoulder. She didn't answer.

I closed my eyes, caressing her skin with my lips. "I'm sorry I called you a slut."

She shivered and let a long sigh escape her lips. Needing to ensure she understood, I continued my monologue.

"I'm just a stupid man. A jealous man. The thought of other guys . . . inside you. It nearly broke me." Fuck. Why did I have the need to confess? I'd never felt guilty before. Why now?

One hand resting on her pussy, the other on her breast, contentment flowed through me. This was exactly where I wanted to be—who I wanted to be with. Nobody else would do.

"Please forgive me?"

Her hand slipped over mine, lacing our fingers together and squeezing.

Yes.

Perfect silence filled the space around us. It was only us in that moment. Nothing else existed.

I shut all thoughts out. I didn't want to think, to analyze this. The answers could be more than I could tolerate. I just wanted to soak up this moment—revel in it and forget everything else.

Chapter 25
MAYA

I couldn't speak without giving myself away. Silent tears streamed down my cheeks and into the pillow as he told me all I needed to know.

He doesn't hate me—just like I don't hate him.

Yet confusion rose up in my gut and took hold of my mind. There was no way in hell this could ever work.

I lay in Oliver's arms thinking of all the reasons this was fucked up. My father was married to his mother—in society's eyes we were family. Step *siblings*. Although we weren't related by blood, we were supposed to be a family like any other. I got that.

And then there was Larissa. Oliver's mother really didn't like me. Every time Daddy mentioned how much I looked like my mother, she'd glare at me through narrowed eyes. When I was fifteen I'd nearly cut my locks and bleached my hair to look more like her so that she wouldn't see me as such a threat. But then my Quinn pointed out that it would make it worse. I'd be a younger blonde—a younger version of herself, and she'd hate me even more.

I just couldn't win, so I stayed who I was—it was just easier being me, although my appearance was clearly something most other people in my family abhorred. Even my grandmother had told daddy that she couldn't look at me without seeing her daughter, and that seeing me made her sad. It sucked being me.

Oliver King was one of the only people, other than my father, who'd ever told me I was beautiful. It made my heart smile. I wanted to be beautiful to him, just like he was the most beautiful creature on the planet to me. I couldn't look at him without my body feeling hot and bothered, my heart racing, my palms sweating. It was good to know I had the same effect on him.

But when he called me a slut, it cut deep. The irony was that all the times he'd caught me with other boys it was simply a futile attempted to get him out of my system.

Whenever Oliver was with another girl, rage and jealousy swarmed my body, driving me to the edge of insanity. It made me do crazy things to force him to see me. Things I'd never normally do. No other boy had seen me completely naked. Or watched me touch myself. I'd reserved that for Oliver only.

God, I was naïve.

I wanted to curl into a ball and hide from him. Yet when he put his arms around me and pulled me to his chest, calmness washed over me. The dull ache in my heart slowly subsided. I felt safe. Wanted. At peace.

Oliver's even breathing behind my back and the weight of his arm around me made the corners of my mouth twitch. He'd dozed off, holding me tightly against his chest.

Lifting his arm, I turned slowly so as not to wake him. This was the perfect opportunity to really study his face. Usually I could only steal glimpses when he wasn't looking, or stare at photos of him. Having him up close and personal was an unexpected delight.

I reached up to stroke his cheek. The rough stubble under my fingertips made my pussy clench thinking of his face between my legs, the way it had burned when he'd been eating me out. Oh God, I wanted him there again. So, so badly.

The tip of my finger traced the lines etched at the corners of his eyes. I loved when he smiled and it lit up his eyes, making small crinkles on his face. I stretched to softly kiss the end of his perfect nose—straight and proud, like the man he was. He reminded me of a picture of a prince I'd seen as a kid in one of the fairy tales I loved to read.

I mused at how gorgeous his face was while he was sleeping. Gone were the frown lines I'd become accustomed to. His lips curled into a small smile and it simply delighted me that they could do something other than twist into a smirk when I was around.

Unable to stop myself, my finger moved down his torso onto forbidden territory. Oh God, how often had I wanted to bleach my eyeballs for drinking in the deep V that sat just above where his pants usually hung low on his hips? I giggled softly as he moaned when my fingertips brushed over the trail of hair running south from his belly. My eyes widened as his cock, which up until now had lain soft between us, stiffened. My mouth watered as I imagined what he would taste like. I'd only ever had one cock in my mouth, and Oliver had been too quick to put a stop to it that day on the stairwell.

Still asleep, he nudged his erection into my belly, his hardness pushing into my skin and setting me alight. If this was the only time I ever got to be with him, I simply had to taste him.

Sweet Lord, this was so wrong, yet so damn right. Rubbing my thumb gently over his tip, spreading his pre-cum around the head, he instinctively turned to lie on his back so that his stiff cock lay on his flat stomach. He was perfection.

Pushing my hair back from my face, I leaned over, licking just the tip of his erection to taste him. Just as I thought—amazing. My lips curled around his dick, my tongue swirling around the rim, feeling, tasting, learning every inch of him.

Oliver moaned, stretching his limbs, opening his body completely. I smiled as I cupped his balls in my hand, kneading gently. "Jesus, little bee, what have I done to deserve this? For a moment I thought I'd died and gone to heaven."

His raspy voice was sexy as hell, spurring me on to become braver in my actions. I took his girth in my palm, stroking up and down as I sucked the tip. His hand came down on my head, holding me down as he flexed his hips upwards.

"Fuck that's good," he groaned. "Take me deeper."

Smiling, I obeyed, opening my throat until I had all of him in my mouth. I thought I'd gag at the sheer size of his erection, but somehow he slid down with ease as my head bobbed up and down. He hissed through his teeth, then reached for me and pulled me over him.

"Need to come inside your pussy, baby."

He rolled us over until he was pressing me into the mattress, my breasts flattened under his weight. My fingers found their way into his messy hair as I held my breath, waiting for him to possess me. His face was soft with sleep and sex, his eyes deep pools that bore into mine. For the first time I saw something there I'd never seen before. It stole my breath away. But before I could put a name to it, he spoiled it all by talking.

Grinning down at me, he said in a hoarse voice, "You *are* a slut. *My* fucking slut. And I fucking love it."

His mouth came crushing down on mine—warm, possessive. I sighed into his mouth, letting him ravage me while my pussy ached for his cock. After a while, he let go of my lips and moved his mouth down my neck, sucking and licking as he went.

"Baby, you fucking ruin me," he grunted as his mouth latched on to a nipple, sucking hard. My back arched off the bed as I unashamedly pushed more of my breast into his mouth.

Once he'd had enough of my breasts, he spread my legs open wide. Jesus. Fuck. The way he grinned as he stared at my wet pussy made me cringe and want to beg at the same time.

"Oliver," I moaned, closing my eyes as heat clawed its way over my chest and face.

"This is the most beautiful pussy I've ever seen. Christ, I've waited so fucking long." He sounded breathless, his heavy eyelashes hooding his eyes so that I couldn't see them.

Reverently, he kissed the insides of my thighs, driving me to the edge. My need for him was escalating by the second. God, I hated being so damn needy.

Long, languid strokes licked over my quivering pussy. My legs trembled so much I had to hold on to them. His tongue circled my clit with such finesse that my back lifted completely off the mattress and I screamed his name.

Now I understood why all those girls were so noisy. Oliver was an expert at making a woman come hard. I never wanted him to taste another pussy as long as I lived. I only wanted him to crave mine.

Chuckling softly, he crept up the bed till his rock hard dick lay flat on my stomach. My eyes fluttered open and I watched as it throbbed and jerked a few times, pre-cum spilling from the tip.

Fuck me! Please, please fuck me! I wanted to scream, but I just lay there, unable to utter a word, eyes wide, licking my lips, remembering his taste. Oliver King could fuck me all day long. Any way he wanted, whenever he wanted, however he wanted. And I'd be begging for more.

Craving him inside me.

Craving him.

Eyes squeezed shut, shame washed over me for wanting this man so much that it hurt. My illicit desire was burning through me like a wildfire and there was nothing I could do to stop it. Nothing I wanted to do to stop it.

My heart beat so loudly in my ears I was sure it would explode at any moment.

He moved against me, pushing his cock into me as if I would break. I never expected tenderness from my stepbrother. Never expected him to be so damn gentle. It undid me in ways I couldn't fathom.

"Open your eyes, little bee. I want to see you when you come."

See me? All these years I believed I was invisible to him and now he wanted to see me—every bit of me, from my dripping wet pussy to inside the depths of my soul. He was unraveling me; slowly, surely, ruining me for anyone else. There was no way I could ever be satisfied by another man. No way I could let another man touch me or fuck me like he did.

Yes, I was my stepbrother's slut. And that's exactly the way I wanted it to be.

For now.

Chapter 26
OLIVER

Pain would bind us.

It wasn't her fault. The rage that burned inside my gut had settled there long before I knew of her existence. Yet, in a twisted way, I wanted her to suffer, to feel the hurt as much as I did.

Love was for fairy tales, chick flicks, and delusional people. After seeing how it fucked up my parent's life and my own, I wanted no part of such a fallacy. All it brought was heartache and self-doubt. I could live without that shit in my life.

I never had illusions where Maya was concerned. She was nothing more than a pleasurable pastime, my dark obsession driven by desire and lust. These emotions I could handle.

Complications like trust and commitment and loyalty weren't in my vocabulary—unless they described my innate desire for control. Although I wasn't prepared to give them to anyone, in all things related to Maya, I expected—no, demanded—these elements from her.

I took from her, bled her dry, never getting enough, always demanding more. The more she gave, the more I wanted. Relentless in my pursuit of nirvana, although I had no fucking idea what it looked like.

Pushing comfort zones, taking risks.

In-fucking-satiable.

Until I broke her.

Only then would I rest.

Why I had this fucked-up need for her, I didn't know—but fuck if I wasn't going to stop analyzing it and follow through on it instead.

"On your knees, baby," I commanded. "Tonight I'm claiming your ass."

We'd just had a shower together, and her lips were still swollen from sucking my cock under the streaming water. I'd wrapped a towel around her and carried her to the bedroom, carefully depositing her onto the cushions on the floor.

"Oliver, I . . . I'm not sure I can handle that," she said hesitantly as her skin turned a shade of blush.

I raised an eyebrow. "Seems I'll have to call on Bianca then. My cock needs ass tonight."

She sucked in a breath. "You're cruel," she hissed. "Don't you have a fucking heart?"

"Baby, either you give me your ass, or I find it elsewhere. Simple, really." She was testing me. Every fucking time I wanted something from her she resisted me. My patience was wearing thin. "And to answer your question: no. I was born without a heart. They're a hindrance. More lives have been lost through war and other horrors than through natural disasters because idiots tried to follow their fucking hearts."

Maya narrowed her eyes and glared at me. "Yeah, I believe you. You're a heartless monster. Incapable of feelings if they aren't connected to your dick. How do you live with yourself, Oliver? How do you look into your own eyes in a mirror?"

I smirked. "Why the fuck would I want to do that? Look into my own eyes? That's for pussies and new-age wimps." I removed the towel from around her body, my gaze drinking in her nakedness and sizing up her perfect backside. "What's it going to be? Are you getting on your fucking knees and surrendering?"

"Call Bianca. You can do to her what you want; I don't care." Her chin lifted in defiance.

Christ. My cock stiffened to a painful level. Little bee knew how to push my fucking buttons. It just made me want her more when she denied me.

Something in me snapped. She'd called my bluff. I was right where I wanted to be. With her.

"No. It's not her I want. *You*. I want you and I'm taking what I want, and you're going to give it up willingly because I know you want me too."

"Make me," she hissed. "You have no shame, no decency—just taking from me because you've blackmailed me into it."

"Therein lies the pleasure, my dear. The harder you fight me, and the harder I have to work for it, the more I'm going to enjoy fucking you."

Time for talk had ended. Grabbing a fist full of her hair, I pushed her forward so that she was forced to brace herself with her hands on the carpet to stop herself from face planting.

Opening the night stand drawer, I removed the new flogger I'd bought earlier and ran it through my fingers. I loved the smell of new leather as it drifted to my nostrils. Something about it made me horny as fuck. Leather mixed with cunt juice was even better.

Maya's eyes widened as she took in the chocolate brown flogger. I loved watching her squirm. From beneath her lashes she stared up at me, her lips wet and slightly parted. Turned on in spite of her protests. Her nipples were hard as fucking stone and I could smell her arousal from here. She was dripping wet and I hadn't even touched her.

"Ass in the air," I commanded, "legs wide open." I wanted to see her dripping wet pussy; I wanted to let the aroma of it fill the whole fucking room. I wished I could bottle that shit—I'd never have to work again a day in my life.

The flogger connected to her flesh. Dark pink lines appeared on her smooth-as-silk skin. Fuck. I could come just looking at it.

She gritted her teeth, refusing to make a sound. Holy fuck if that didn't make me wild. Other women would've moaned in pleasure and pain. Not my little bee. Withholding her sounds from me as punishment was driving me to the fucking edge. I wanted to hear her moan, hear her cry out. She denied me.

Lashing the flogger at her, I made sure it connected to her pussy lips as well, sending her a clear message not to fuck with me. Shuddering, she whimpered and closed her knees together, hiding her pussy from me.

"The more you resist, the more it's turning me the fuck on, Maya. Keep it up, baby, cause my cock is going to ride your ass so hard it's going to make your eyes water."

Slowly her knees slid sideways, exposing her sex again. It was so fucking swollen—juice ran down her legs—that I salivated for a taste of her on my tongue.

"Jesus, little bee, you're fucking loving this. You're so ready to be fucked—your pussy is dripping wet."

Reveling in the fact that I would be the first man to enter her ass, I rolled a condom onto my erect cock with trembling hands.

"Lean forward on the cushions, baby, arms behind your back," I grunted, the veins on my cock showing through the transparent condom.

She hesitated, just as I expected. Gripping the back of her neck, I pushed her forward until her elbows were on the cushions and her ass was in my face. Leaning over, I grabbed both her arms and pulled them back, then fastened them with the leather belt I'd placed within reach.

"Oliver, *please*," she begged.

Was she begging for my cock, or for me to let her go? Either way, I was beyond caring. The big brain was beyond thinking rationally. I rubbed my palms over her ass, feeling her soft skin and the welts from the flogger. I licked over the red, soothing the burning skin with my cool tongue until it glistened in the light.

With both hands, I spread her ass cheeks open. My heartbeat throbbed in my cock and my mouth went dry. Virgin ass was the best. I went in for the kill. I licked her pussy, sucking her juices with slurping sounds, flicking her clit with my tongue until she cried out.

"Oh God," she moaned, "*Oliver.*" Her chest heaved and her breath came in short, sharp bursts as an orgasm hit her. Smiling against her skin, my tongue licked her hole, wetting her for my cock. She was ready. Finally. I could hardly contain my dick.

Slowly nudging into her, I felt her stiffen, so I pulled back slightly. I eased my cock in, sliding it in inch by inch, allowing her to adjust every time I went deeper. Moments later, she'd taken my whole cock up her ass without a problem. I was ready to fuck. Slowly at first, I controlled my movements with quaking breath until I felt her body relax.

There was no holding back. I fucked her ass, tight and warm and just fucking perfect, until I couldn't hold my orgasm back any longer. I pulled out and ripped the condom off, fisted my cock and watched my cum spill over her ass cheeks and crack. *Jesus fuck.*

Satisfied that I'd made her submit, made her say my name as she came, I rolled her to her side and spooned into her back.

Her ass was mine. Slowly I was claiming every part of her. Slowly she was becoming my possession, whether she liked it or not. I ran my hands over her ample ass cheeks, loving the feel of their provocative plumpness under my skin.

Little bee was all I expected her to be—and more.

Fuck, this woman blew my mind. Even though she didn't know it yet, she was my alter ego in so many ways it scared the shit out of me.

Chapter 27
MAYA

Sipping on a cool drink, I spread out on a lounge chair and watched the sun set over the ocean. It was one of the things I loved most about the house—spectacular ocean views meant breathtaking sunsets.

It was the first Friday night I'd get to spend all alone and I loved the idea of lounging around the pool, eating pizza for dinner, and just relaxing. My father and Larissa had gone away for the weekend to visit her sister in Vancouver and my dearest stepbrother had business in LA.

As dusk settled, the solar-powered lights came on and turned the garden into a fairy wonderland. Spotlights lit up giant palm trees and I watched a swarm of bugs swirl around the main light hidden between the foliage. The distant croak of a frog and the chirping of a few birds were all the sounds to be heard. I smiled to myself, completely content being alone. *Peace and tranquility at last.*

I jumped into the pool and swam my usual number of laps—plus an extra ten to build my stamina. I needed it with Oliver around. The man was demanding both mentally and physically, and I had to keep my mind sharp and my body fit.

Because it was warm and balmy, I stripped out of my bikini and rinsed the chlorine from my skin and hair under the outdoor shower. Not bothering to dry myself, I simply wrapped a sarong around my body and tied it at my boobs before I settled back onto the chair with my drink. Ice tinkled against the frosty glass as I took a long sip. With the remote, I turned on the stereo and seconds later the crooning voice of Michael Bublé floated across the lush lawn.

I flicked through my e-reader and tried to read the romance novel I'd been dying to finish, but my eyelids grew heavy and eventually even the tablet became too weighty to hold up. I closed my eyes and gave in to slumber, completely relaxing for the first time in weeks.

Through my hazy brain I became aware of a warm sensation creeping up my leg. Oh God, I hated crawling insects. My eyes flew open as I leaned forward to swat the intruder off my leg. Startled I stared into big brown eyes, glistening in the moonlight, as they smiled up at me.

"Shhh, little bee, lie back and relax." His voice was like golden honey: soft, warm, and soothing. Hypnotizing.

Was I dreaming? Oliver wasn't supposed to be back yet.

With a small smile twisting the corners of my mouth, I settled back into the cushions, wanting this dream to carry on. Sweet, smiling Oliver only lived in dreamland. Of that I was pretty sure.

Strong, warm hands pushed my legs apart so that the sarong fell open. A wet tongue licked up the insides of the sensitive skin of my thighs, the pressure just enough to make me whimper softly. This was fast becoming my favorite dream. The tongue ran up one leg and stopped as it reached my apex, then moved to the other leg to repeat the action.

My pussy clenched, wanting part of the tongue's action. And, as in all good dreams, I didn't have to wait long. A long sigh left my body as the tongue found my clit and circled slowly, hands traveling up my thighs to my hips. My legs fell open wider, granting the tongue access to my core, wanting more of the delicious assault.

Two fingers found their way inside my warmth, making me squirm with pure delight.

"Ahhh," I sighed, falling deeper and deeper under the tongue's spell. Fingers rhythmically plunged in and out, working me up to a heightened state of pleasure. The fingers withdrew and I heard clinking of ice against glass.

A few seconds later an icy sensation crawled across my skin, causing me to shiver. My nipples peaked into tight hard nubs. Warm lips traced the wet icy trail up my thighs, over my stomach, and rimmed my belly button before making large circles around the outsides of my breasts. It was unlike anything I'd experienced before. Fire and ice on my skin.

"Yes," I hissed, every nerve ending alive. One nipple assaulted by ice, the other by a hot mouth that was sucking hard.

My hands moved forward and tried to touch the face that belonged to the mouth, but as suddenly as it had appeared it was gone. Before I could voice my disappointment, I heard more ice clinking, so I just lay back and waited.

A gasp escaped my lips as wet coldness slipped between the lips of my pussy, causing my body to jerk. And then, to the sound of the softest chuckle, the coldness slipped inside me along with two fingers. At the same time, warm lips sucked on my clit. I was going to explode. I lifted my hips and rode the face between my thighs, wanton and needy, chasing an orgasm.

Seconds later, the warm tongue speared my insides, fucking me with vigor, replacing the cold with wet warmth.

"Oh God," I screamed, spiraling out of control. White light flashed across my vision and my body started to convulse as an almighty orgasm hit me.

And then, when I thought I could take no more, the warm lips descended on mine and kissed me, sucking my breath away, possessing every cell in my body. I didn't care that it was only a dream—it was one of the most beautiful experiences of my life.

Sensual and electric, love crackled in the air.

The deep voice drifted toward me. "Little bee, I'm going to fuck you now."

I felt his warmth over me. His body radiated heat as a hard cock found my entrance and slid inside.

Rocking his hips back and forth, then with circular motions, the cock inside filled me until I could feel or think of nothing else but the sensation of it as it moved inside me.

"Little bee, my love," a voice rasped on the wind.

Oh dream maker, never let this end.

"Come with me, love."

I did. I let go and found release as his cock found its at the same time.

Perfect unison. Perfect synchronization.

The warm body covered mine, his heart beating wildly under my fingertips. I kept my eyes closed—fear convinced me that the apparition would melt if I opened them.

After a while my breathing settled and I slipped into a deeper sleep, safe in the arms of my lover. I felt protected. Secure.

Loved.

I woke what must've been hours later. I'd been lifted from the chair and was being carried inside the house. Forcing my eyes open, I smiled up at Oliver.

"Hey you," I said dreamily, "when did you get back? I wasn't expecting you."

"I just got here a short while ago. I went up to the bedroom and saw you down by the pool from the window, so I came down to get you." A small frown sat between his brows.

"I dreamed about you," I said, my mind still in another world I didn't want to leave.

"Yeah? Was it good?"

"Yeah," I whispered into his chest. *"The best."*

Chapter 28
MAYA

I was exhausted. Lack of sleep and fucking all night long for days on end had taken its toll. Oliver was insatiable. He came for me when he wanted, where he wanted. However he wanted.

He was possessive. Demanding. I'd become Oliver's willing plaything, his fuck toy. At night when everyone had gone to bed, I'd be summoned to his room, or he'd appear in my bathroom while I was soaking in the tub or taking a shower.

He was moody and angry all the time, as if he had to prove something to himself. What happened to the sweet guy I'd given my virginity to? Maybe I'd dreamed all of that. With every passing day, I saw him get more distant and relentless in the way he fucked me.

My life had changed so much since my stepbrother had found me in the bathroom bleeding on the floor that it was divided distinctly into two parts: *Before Oliver and After Oliver*.

Before Oliver had become a blur. The only highlights were the times my dad or Oliver were featured in some small part. The rest I'd forgotten.

After Oliver had taken over my existence. I'd become addicted to the man I'd always pretended to hate. It didn't matter how badly he treated me, I took it every single time and then came back for more.

Since he brought me home from the clinic, he'd moved into the house, working from the study. Larissa seemed pleased to have her son so close after all the years she'd hardly seen him.

"So I can watch over you, little bee. Make sure you never try to leave me again," he'd said when I questioned him about not going back to LA.

Since that first time when I'd given him my virginity, he'd fucked me on every conceivable space in the house. He'd dragged me down to the kitchen in the middle of the night, saying he was hungry. He was—hungry for me. The fact we could be found out at any moment spiked my adrenaline, made it even more thrilling.

He started with my pussy, then slowly trained my ass. Oliver had a thing for fucking my ass. And I'd do anything to please him, even wear butt plugs to college to stretch me enough so I was ready for his cock later. It made sitting through lectures pure torture, yet it also excited me; I had a constant reminder of where he'd been inside me and where he was going to be the next time he screwed me.

Sometimes he couldn't wait and he'd show up at college on the pretense that I'd left a book on the kitchen table or some other bullshit story. Sometimes I'd see Oliver walking up the path and pretend I didn't see him, letting the boy I was chatting to come a little too close to me or even brush against my shoulder.

Funny how boys liked rubbing their shoulders or legs against mine. It did nothing for me, except give me the ability to watch Oliver's face as he glared at the boy, wanting to rip him apart with his bare teeth. Some part of me found pleasure in knowing that I could inflict such torture on him, just as he'd done to me for all those years.

It turned me on so much that my pussy started weeping, the aroma of my sex so strong that even the innocent boy would sense something different and start panting. It was risky, yet I couldn't stop myself, wanting to spur Oliver's jealousy to fever pitch so he'd fuck me even harder when we were finally alone.

"Has any boy been checking out my tits today?" he'd ask as he grabbed both my breasts in his palms and squeezed 'til I wanted to cry out. I'd shake my head, biting down on my lip to stop a smile from giving me away, inwardly pleased that he was so possessive and so damn insanely jealous. I needed my daily fix of Oliver's cock, my attachment to him growing more and more, my dependency on him reaching dangerous levels.

Oliver was my drug of choice.

I never denied him.

We fucked like bunnies in the springtime, neither of us ever having enough. It got to the point that I needed a nap most days when he left the house for a jog; sometimes he'd go to LA for business meetings so I could get some much needed sleep.

In some part I hated myself for the way I couldn't resist him. Hated how he always won in the end. Why, when it came to Oliver, was I so damn stupid sometimes? He was slowly but surely breaking any resistance I had to him.

Quinn was worried about me. She said it was unhealthy not wanting to do or be anywhere if it didn't involve Oliver. I just smiled at her, knowing she'd never understand what it felt like—I only felt alive when he was around. There was no use in defending myself.

Sometimes Oliver was sweet and caring—those were the times I breathed for. I was so damn confused I gave up trying to figure him out.

Consumed. It was the only way I could describe my situation. I held on to every moment because I never knew when it would end. Because one thing I did know: this couldn't last. We'd kill one another fucking the way we did.

Sweaty. Dirty. Always pushing for more.

Chapter 29
OLIVER

I sat at my desk and scratched my head. Having Maya in my bed was fine—as long as nobody was aware of it. The mansion my mother lived in was large enough that she and her husband occupied a completely separate wing than Maya and me. And we were careful to never be together when the servants were in our part of the house. All hell would break loose if anyone found out about us. We were doomed from the start and it was a fucking nightmare to try to figure out how I was going to handle this.

Alec hated scandal of any sort. His first wife's suicide had nearly ruined his reputation in the medical industry and the high society circles he moved in. Everyone judged him, blamed him for the loss of her life. How had he not read the signs and stopped it from happening?

The man would go ape-shit crazy if he had any idea I was fucking his daughter. Nearly two weeks of wild abandon and fucking Maya as often as I could, under my stepfather's roof, was already taking its toll on my nerves. And hers. Sometimes she'd cry after we fucked, telling me that this had to end. I wouldn't listen. I didn't want to hear it.

The real estate agent had just delivered the documents for the purchase of a home on the hill of Santa Barbara. I couldn't go back to my empty life in LA. No amount of working hard and fucking even harder could cure my obsession with my stepsister.

Nor could I stay in my stepfather's house any longer. I was unable to keep my hands off Maya, fucking her from the moment we went upstairs to my room after dinner until dawn, not to mention every opportunity I found during the day. But the things I still wanted to do to her, the ways I needed to take her, were impossible while staying there.

My little bee was sweet and smart. She knew just how to wrap me around her little finger. Christ. All this time I thought I was the one in control, but it was her all along. I was acting like a fucking lovesick teenager—she invaded my every waking moment. If she wasn't with me, I'd be thinking about her, getting hard remembering her taste, dreaming about her. My dark obsession with my stepsister ran so fucking deep there was no way I wanted to stop this. Yet I knew we were on a collision course with destiny.

It ate at me like cancer, causing me sleepless nights and anxiety. In the small hours of the night, when Maya curled up in my arms with my dick still inside her, I'd make up my mind to give her up, to walk away. But the instant my eyes met hers when she awoke, I fucking couldn't do it. I couldn't walk away. In fact, I craved her more. My hunger for her grew in intensity until I was convinced I was losing my fucking mind.

Some day everything would fall apart. Destroy us. It terrified me that we could be torn apart by shit beyond our control. I fucking hated the despair it left in my gut. Hated that I was waiting for it to come smashing down around us.

But more than anything, I hated that I'd become weak. I'd allowed her to get under my fucking skin. It had to stop. She was nothing more than dirty sex to me. It was her gorgeous body I wanted to fuck, nothing more. My obsession was purely carnal.

Raw.

Primal.

But that was it.

I needed to take back my fucking power. Prove that I hadn't become soft because of her fucking pussy driving me wild. God forbid that I fell in love with her. My *own* stepsister. What kind of man would that make me if sex wasn't the only thing on my mind?

A deviant.

A fucking depraved deviant.

Maya needed to understand this was only about sex. *Nothing more.*

We couldn't fall in love with one another.

It was the one thing that would break us.

Force us apart.

Love.

Anger swirled in my gut that I'd allowed her to have pleasure from this. I was losing my perspective on what this was all about. This was revenge for all the wrongs that had been done to me. And since I'd already taken her virginity, there was nothing to stop me from showing her just how rotten I was at the core of my soul.

I was going to fuck her, make her scream with pain. The same pain I felt deep in the abysses of my fucking soul.

Was I heartless? Yes. Yes, I fucking was.

And Maya would find out all about that soon enough.

Once I'd exorcised my demons, then I'd consider letting her go. I'd use her then throw her away. Discard her like a broken toy. Because that was what she was. A sex toy for my pleasure. I wanted to believe it.

Then why did it hurt so fucking much whenever I thought of my life without her? Why was I miserable when I was away from her? Why did every cell in my fucking body yearn for her?

I hated myself for feeling this way.

Before, I had the power in my hands. Now I was weak for her. I needed her like I needed air. Something wasn't right. I had to fix it.

Grabbing the keys of my SUV, I made my way to my car. She'd be at class now, but luckily I knew the campus, so I'd track her down. I'd teach her that I was her master. That I hadn't become soft. That I would only use her. That I didn't need her to breathe.

That love was a four letter word.

Twenty minutes later, I'd found a parking spot near the building where I knew she was taking her class. I walked over the lush green lawns, asking a few people that I'd recognized and seen with Maya before if they knew where she was.

"Yeah, she's in that building," the brunette whose name I'd forgotten said, checking me out with big eyes running up and down my body. She looked at her watch. "Her class finishes in fifteen minutes. Why don't you come to the cafeteria with us while you wait? She usually comes there after class."

I followed her and her friend to a glass building with tables set outside. We found an empty one and sat down. I wasn't really listening to their conversation; I kept looking at my watch.

"You're Maya's stepbrother, aren't you?" The blonde cocked her head and twirled her locks between her fingers—the universal sign for subtle flirting.

"Yeah. Why?"

"Um, we heard you moved to LA. Pity you didn't come to this school."

I didn't feel like explaining myself to them. There really wasn't any point. The second I spotted Maya, I'd be gone.

"Ah, there they come now," the brunette chirped.

My head snapped up. *They?*

Sure as fucking hell, Maya came toward the building, oblivious that I was there. She was laughing, completely at ease with the guy she was with. My gaze shifted to him, ready to tear his head off. I sucked in a breath—it was none other than the little prick I'd thrown out only the other week. What the fuck?

Unable to watch any longer as he laid his hand on her arm and smiled into her eyes, I jumped up and stormed toward her. As I approached, the fucker saw me first. His eyes widened and he stopped talking, his mouth gaping open as I closed in on them.

"Maya, I need you to come with me," I growled. "And you, jackass, quit touching her. I've warned you before. Don't make me fucking break your dick."

I didn't wait for his response. I grabbed hold of her arm and pulled her back toward the building she'd come from.

"Oliver, wait. What the fuck's gotten into you?" Maya said, digging her heels in and refusing to come along.

"If you don't want me to throw you over my fucking shoulder and carry you off, you better come along," I grunted. Her resistance was pissing me off big time.

"Stop acting like a fucking barbarian." Her voice had a panicked tone to it. "Everyone is looking at us, for fuck sake. Slow the fuck down and act normal.'"

Jesus fucking Christ, I was going to burst into hysterical laughter. Normal? I didn't have a fucking clue what that was. *Normal* was not in my vocabulary.

"The bathroom. Where is it?" My patience was fraying. Any minute I was going to snap.

"You're going crazy because you need to take a piss? What the hell?" she said, indignation clear in her tone.

I laughed. It was the safest of all the options. I saw the board pointing to the unisex bathrooms and pulled her inside, locking the door behind us. I didn't wait for another word from her; I slammed her hard against the wall, my mouth closing over hers. I caught her gasp in my mouth as I lifted her off the ground, pressing her back into the concrete wall. Maya's legs automatically clasped around my hips, squeezing tightly. Her skirt rode up her thighs; I pushed it up further until the fabric bundled around her waist.

"Got to fuck you," I grunted while loosening my belt and dropping my pants to my ankles. My cock sprang free, hot and throbbing. Anxious to feel her warmth. Gripping both of her wrists in one hand, she whimpered as I pinned them above her head. They'd still be tender, especially since she'd just taken off the bandages, so I squeezed harder, making her cry out in pain.

Good. I wanted her to feel pain. If I felt it, she sure as hell needed to feel it, too.

Pushing her panties to the side, my cock thrust into her all at once. She shuddered from the pressure of taking all of me to the hilt. Fucking her like an animal, I thrust in and out, harder and faster, not caring if she liked it or not.

This was for me. To show her who owned her. That I was her master.

Her whimpering became louder, but I covered her mouth with my hand as I fucked her into next week. My eyes met hers. Large. Frightened. *Dilated.*

A dead fucking giveaway that she *liked* this. Fuck. I was using her and she was fucking turned on. Little bee was as fucked-up as I was.

I tore my gaze away and bit into her shoulder. A muffled scream escaped her lips as my teeth and cock sank ruthlessly into her, claiming her.

And then I came. I came so hard that my knees nearly buckled under me.

Tears splashed onto her cheeks as I took her mouth with mine, possessing her completely.

When my rage finally subsided and I pulled away from her mouth, she blinked a few times and turned her head away from me. I gripped her cheeks roughly and jerked her head back to me.

"Never look away from me, Maya. Never," I warned through gritted teeth.

Her tear-stained face turned red, her eyes blazing as she spat in my face.

"You, Oliver King, are a fucking monster. I despise you."

My hand tightened around her throat.

"And you, Maya Childs, are *my* little slut. Deal with it."

I stepped back from her, letting her feet slide back to the floor. Pulling up my pants, I fastened the clasp of my belt.

"If I see that prick touching you again, you are both going to be sorry."

Shaking, I stormed out of the washroom, never looking back.

I was an asshole. When it came to Maya, I couldn't help myself.

Chapter 30
MAYA

Oliver left me there like a rag doll. The way he used me cut through me like a knife.

I could handle most things he threw my way—the rough sex, the mean names. But what I couldn't stand was Oliver cutting me off without explanation—cold and outright rejection. Like him avoiding me for weeks on end.

Being abandoned was my worst fear. The total opposite of my deepest heart's desire to belong wholeheartedly to someone.

Sometimes I made myself believe that I could feel a connection between Oliver and me beyond the mind-blowing sex. That we were bonded, not just by sex, nor blood, because we weren't related, but by something far greater than the two of us.

But as quickly as elation and acceptance had started breaking my resistance down, my walls shot right back up again when he treated me the way he just had. My heart had slowly started cracking open as I'd seen slivers of what life with Oliver could be like. Sometimes he was tender and caring to a fault, only to treat me like dirt the next time he fucked me.

Rag dolls had it good. They were loved by their owners. Mine just used me and then cast me aside. Didn't care what happened to me afterwards. And it hurt like fuck. So after each episode, I'd build the wall around my heart back up again, only this time a few layers higher, a few layers deeper.

Impenetrable. Unfeeling. That's what I wanted to be.

Instead it was breaking me—each time a little more. One day I'd run, I'd say no to the bullshit and get the hell out of there. If only my fucking addiction weren't as paralyzing. If only I didn't need it more than my freedom.

Since I'd started college, I was focusing more on my studies. And I'd learned to cope with everything thrown my way. But rejection was the hardest pill to swallow. It shredded my insides, made me bleed.

Worse than any blade I'd ever pushed against my skin.

Deeper than the sharpest edge.

"Maya, what the fuck?" Quinn pushed the door open and stared at me. I just sat there, my back against the cold wall, tears streaming unchecked down my cheeks. I didn't care who saw me like this. Nothing could hurt me more than Oliver King already had.

Trust Quinn to find me. She was like a damn bloodhound. Thank God.

"Sweetheart, let me help you up." She leaned over and placed her arm undermine and pulled me up slowly. My knees were trembling so hard, I wasn't sure I could stand on my own.

"You don't have to talk. I can just imagine what happened. Oliver fucking King stormed past me like a fucking tornado was on his tail. That man is possessed by the devil. Calling him a monster is kind." Quinn was pissed off. More than I'd ever seen. Her face was flushed and her eyes blazed. I pitied anyone who got in her way when she was this mad. She didn't take shit from any man.

"I'm okay," I lied.

"Seriously, Bee, Oliver would be wise to stay the hell out of my way. Some days I just want to slap some sense into him. He's the biggest asshole I've ever known, and that's saying a lot."

"Yeah, you're right. Maybe Daddy is right, maybe I should be more into Gerard. At least he treats right, not like . . . Oliver." I broke down and sobbed.

Quinn pulled me into her embrace, holding me as I cried on her shoulder. Sobs racked my body as I let it all out. All the anger, all the humiliation, all the hurt, and all the desolation I'd felt for the longest time came to a head and demanded to be addressed.

When I finally stopped, I wiped the snot with the back of my hand and washed it away under the tap. I splashed my face with cold water, welcoming the coolness on my warm skin.

"Gerard, help me get Maya to my car," Quinn called out. All this time he'd been waiting outside, too scared to come in. But at least he stayed, at least he wanted to see that I was okay.

Unlike Oliver.

Chapter 31
OLIVER

I felt like the lowest of low creatures the way I'd left Maya at the campus. Something had taken over my fucking mind and made me crazy. Maybe I did inherit my father's crazy genes after all.

I'd stormed away from the campus, flying past her best friend and the prick I'd nearly knocked over on my way to my car. Roaring away, hitting the gas as hard as I could, I didn't stop until I pulled up outside my condo in LA.

Quinn will step in and take care of Maya. At least she had her best friend to lean on.

I wasn't worthy of Little Bee. Damaged and flawed and so fucked up, I brought her nothing but heartache and pain, so the further I stayed away, the better for her.

Yet it was killing me to stay away. I wanted to go back and grovel at her feet. Beg her to forgive me. Tormented, I hadn't slept properly since I'd left. I couldn't focus on anything and it affected my work. Even my usual healthy appetite had waned and I'd taken up drinking instead.

I'd been back in LA for a week. I'd tried to call Maya several times, but how could I explain to her what had happened if I didn't even know myself? I was bad news, not worthy of her. She'd probably never forgive me. And I couldn't say I'd be surprised.

Another week passed and still I hadn't spoken to her. I'd sent Quinn a text message to find out if Maya was okay—the words she wrote back nearly made me choke when I read them. According to Quinn, if I valued my life and my balls, I'd stay right where I was.

I'd fucked up. Truly fucked up this time.

As the weeks passed my heart grew heavier and heavier. My new boss called me in to his office to talk with me about the mistakes I had been making. It was ridiculous; I always took extreme pride in the quality of my work. But lately I had a bad attitude about everything.

I just didn't give a flying fuck.

Not about work, not about food, not about what I looked like. My three-week-old stubble started to look more like a beard every day.

My boss' words played through my mind as I stared at my bloodshot eyes in the mirror.

"Get a grip, Oliver. When you interviewed for this position we had fifteen other candidates that were equally as qualified as you. The reason we chose you was because of your dynamic personality. And fuck me if I can see a trace of that since you started here."

Those words had hit me hard. My life was turning to shit in front of my eyes.

I couldn't take it anymore. Ironically the real estate agent had called that morning to tell me that my offer on the place in Santa Barbara had gone through and the sale was being finalized in a few weeks.

It was a sign that I had to get my shit together. I had to face Maya and talk to her, even if I had to do it through Quinn; Maya still refused to speak to me. She hadn't taken any of my calls or answered any of my messages in three weeks.

At first it pissed me off, and my messages reflected that. Then, after a while, the hole in my heart became so big; I just wanted to hear her damn voice, even if it was her telling me to fuck off. She'd turned her voicemail off, meaning that I couldn't even leave messages any longer. It sucked.

It had to change. I had to get myself face-to-face with Maya. Quinn told me that she was, in fact, doing remarkably well. Was she forgetting about me already? Had she hooked up with somebody else? The prick from college?

It was time to take action. To step the fuck up and get my life back on track. Show Maya, and myself, that I wasn't a complete loser. That in spite of the stupidity of my actions, I still wanted her.

Because if I'd realized anything, I'd realized how fucking empty my life was without her in it. Not just the sex either. I missed everything about her—the way she bit into her lip when she was shy or apprehensive, the way she rolled her eyes when I was being overbearing, the way she looked up at me when she sucked my dick, and especially the way her face looked like a fucking angel when she slept in my arms.

I knew what I had to do. I had to clean up my act and get my ass over there. Ten minutes later, I stepped out of the shower and dried myself off, dressing in jeans and a tight black t-shirt.

As I drove through the familiar streets back to where I planned to move once again, I formulated a plan. It all fell into place—it finally made sense. First off, I'd tell everyone that I was moving to Santa Barbara permanently. At least Mom would be happy about that. With a job in IT, I could work from anywhere in the world as long as I had Internet access and a computer. I'd just have to get to LA every few weeks to catch up with meetings and report my progress on major projects.

One and a half hours later, I stopped in front of the house. I got out and stretched my legs. I'd worked it all out in my head. I'd ask Maya to forgive me for being such a jackass. I'd make it right with her and we'd carry on where we'd left off. The thought of her refusing me never entered my mind. Little bee needed me as much as I needed her.

Mom greeted me at the door. "Oliver, what a lovely surprise. You've grown a beard!" She reached out and stroked over my cheek. "I wish you'd called before you came though; we're expecting guests tonight."

I was disappointed that Maya hadn't been the one to answer the door, but I'd get to see her soon enough. It was probably best to catch her off guard and in a family environment. That way she wouldn't go crazy on me.

I followed Mom into the house. The aroma of simmering herbs and wine filled the air. "I'm making chicken cacciatore. What are the chances that you show up to one of your favorite dishes?"

"Hmmm . . . good timing. I'm hungry, too." I rubbed my belly, suddenly ravenous.

"You've lost some weight. Working too hard?" she asked, raising an eyebrow as she pinched my cheek as if I were still only five years old.

"Sort of," I lied.

As we reached the dining room, I stopped dead in my tracks. Mom kept babbling on about something, but for the life of me, I couldn't listen to her. All the air sucked out of my lungs as my gaze shifted to where Maya was setting the table. The way she leaned over to place a vase of flowers in the center of the table made my dick ache for her slick warmth.

Fuck, I'd missed her.

"Oliver, you haven't heard a word I said," Mom complained.

"Um, sorry. What was that?" I answered, unable to tear my eyes away from Maya.

"I said we're expecting company tonight. Friends of Alec's. Their son wants to study to be a doctor, so he's going to work at the practice for the holidays. He's keen on Maya too, so sounds to me like a match made in heaven."

Maya's back stiffened. She kept her head down, avoiding my gaze. In fact, she completely ignored me as if I wasn't there.

"Hello, Maya," I offered. She pretended she didn't hear me.

"Maya, please set an extra place for Oliver." She didn't react to Larissa either.

My head swam as I internalized her words. *Maya's boyfriend?* Christ! I thought I'd gotten rid of the little prick weeks ago. *He's a persistent little fucktard, isn't he?* Yet I couldn't blame him. Images of Maya on the stairs that day with his dick in her mouth swarmed my mind. I was going to lose my shit tonight and kill somebody. Trust fucking Alec to hand his daughter over on a plate to the horny little fuck the second I turned my back.

Rage gripped my insides, heat running under the surface of my skin until I was ready to fucking explode. Was Maya playing with me? Was she fucking the college jock who now wanted to be a goddamn doctor so he could get her father's blessing to be in her pants?

"Maya?" I said tersely, struggling to keep my voice even. "Anything you need to tell me?"

She straightened up and stared me in the eye. "No. Why?" Her eyes were cold. Hard. Unrelenting.

"I wasn't aware you had a boyfriend."

"I told you several times," she shrugged and turned her back to me.

Fuck me. She had indeed told me, only I'd thought she was just trying to throw me off. What the fuck had happened since I'd been gone? How could things have changed so drastically in three weeks?

This was way worse than I'd thought. Quinn hadn't been lying when she said Maya was fine. In fact, she was cool as a cucumber—completely impersonal. Nothing like the feisty girl who had tormented my fucking mind.

And all the time I'd thought I was the only one fucking her. *Now she admits to a boyfriend? How long has that been going on?*

The door opened and my stepfather walked in. "Hello, my dear," he said as he kissed my mother on the cheek. "Hey, Maya." He kissed her forehead and lifted his chin to greet me. "Oliver."

He looked mighty pleased with himself, like he'd just won the fucking jackpot. He smiled warmly at my mother. "Our guests will be arriving soon. Let's go have a quiet drink on the patio before they arrive. I'm sure Oliver and Maya can set a table by themselves." He slid his arm around Mom's waist and walked her to the patio door.

As soon as they were out of reach, I leaned toward Maya and whispered in her ear. "You'd better have a fucking good explanation as to what's going on, Maya. I'm not liking this one bit. We have an agreement, remember?"

Suddenly we'd taken ten steps backwards. My mind was in a whirl. Bile rose in my stomach as I placed my hand on her arm.

"What the fuck is going on, little bee?"

Her eyes turned down, staring at the floor. That was never a good sign with Maya. I squeezed her arm—hard.

"I . . . I told you I had a boyfriend before you . . . before we—" She shrugged, her green eyes huge in her face. "You didn't want to listen. As far as Daddy is concerned, Gerard is perfect for me."

"What? Fuck," I said on a heavy exhale. This was blowing my mind.

Her skin had turned paler than I'd ever seen her, even after she'd nearly bled out. She was acting strange—cold as fucking ice. If she screamed at me, hit me, showed some sort of emotion, I'd be able to deal with it a lot better than this.

"Daddy's so excited that Gerard wants to be a doctor. He's taken him under his wing. We'll both be working at the practice during the holidays." Her tone was cheery, as if she were speaking to a stranger.

"Did I not tell you that you were *mine*? Did I not say I wouldn't let another man touch you?" I growled.

She pulled her shoulders back, challenging me. "So what do you want to do, Oliver? Tell my father you've been fucking me blind? *And then what*, Mr. Smartass?"

All the air left my lungs. I couldn't breathe. "Maya, I swear to God, if he fucking touches you, I'm going to cut his balls off and then snap his fucking neck."

Shit just got real. This was as fucked up as fucked up could be.

Chapter 32
MAYA

My grades were slipping and I was struggling to focus in class. Every waking moment I spent thinking of Oliver, wondering what he was doing, convincing myself that I hated his guts, especially after the way he'd abandoned me.

Somehow I'd managed to avoid Gerard since that day on campus. At first it was easy—he'd gone to Europe for two weeks with his parents and I only had to deal with him via texts. His pride was still smarting from the way Oliver had thrown him from the house and treated him in front of everyone on campus. Yet he said it just made him even more determined to be with me.

Of all the nights Oliver chooses tonight to show up?

I'd dreaded this day, and now it was here. I'd tried to tell Gerard that I didn't want to be his girlfriend, but he just laughed it off and said we'd talk when he got back from his trip. He said that he'd forgive my monstrous stepbrother for being such an asshole. How could I explain that the stepbrother I detested and always complained about had become my lover—no, my owner?

"Just play along, and everyone will be happy," I said smiling up at Oliver with confidence I definitely didn't feel. My palms were clammy and my knees trembled—I should've worn pants instead of a damn dress.

"Are you fucking serious? You're going to play along with that? In front of me?" His eyebrows knitted into a deep frown. Oliver King was pissed off and not afraid to show it.

"Just act like the asshole you've always been—that should fool everyone."

"Fuck, little bee, I just want you to know that tonight your ass is going to burn. If he touches you—"

"What then, Oliver? Maybe you should just leave. You're fucking good at it." I tilted my head and stared right through him. "You're the one who is never going to be touching me again, not Gerard."

"Maya. We need to talk."

I didn't want to hear it. "Come to think of it, it may actually be easier on both of us if you just left now."

His jaw clenched a few times and he opened and closed his fists. "Like hell. I'm still planning exactly how I'll snap his dick, and then maybe his neck."

I rolled my eyes. "Always so dramatic, brother dearest."

As much as this charade was tiresome, it was payback for all the times I'd watched his hand disappear under the table when Bianca had slept over. By the expression on her face, the way her lips parted, and the glow on her skin, I always knew *exactly* where Oliver's hand was. It wasn't her knee. Or even her thigh.

"Don't do this, little bee."

"Don't call me that. My name is Maya."

The pained expression on his face made my heart squeeze. I also knew exactly how that felt. Watching and being powerless to do anything about it was one of the worst feelings I'd ever had. Funny how the tables had turned.

Moments later we were joined by Dad, Larissa, and their guests. Gerard beamed from ear to ear when he saw me. He'd picked up about five pounds since I'd last seen him. Grinning, he walked over toward me and pulled me into his embrace, going straight in for a kiss before I had a chance to brace myself. I just barely managed to turn my face in time to feel his lips wet my cheek. His cologne wafted to my nostrils, and although it was probably expensive, it made my stomach turn. There was only one man who could turn me on by the way he smelled alone—and he didn't need cologne to do that to me.

I thought I heard a low growl from behind me, but I couldn't be sure. Really? Oliver was going to go all alpha male here, in front of everyone? Suppressing a nervous giggle, I let Gerard hug me for a moment longer before pulling away.

"Must've been a good trip, Gerard," I said dryly.

"It was, babe, but I missed you," he said, still holding on to both of my arms. "Look at you, all suntanned and lovely."

"*Babe*?" Oliver growled in my ear. Startled, I pulled away completely and went over to greet Gerard's parents.

"Oh, Maya, you have no idea how much our boy missed you. Next time we do a trip, I insist you come along. Gerard is no fun when you aren't around. All he wants to do is sleep and eat. He needs you around to keep him occupied," Mrs. Langford said, smiling.

"Yeah, you should've come along—just like in high school. We could've had sleepovers every night," Gerard said. "I miss those days."

Five pairs of eyebrows shot up virtually at the same time. I laughed, then slapped Gerard's arm. "Silly boy, sleepovers are for kids. Besides, you snore."

My stepbrother nearly choked on the olive he'd just popped into his mouth. I smiled sweetly and, without looking in his direction, I turned on my heels and quickly excused myself to go to the kitchen to check on the dessert I was baking. Every time I opened my damn mouth, I said the wrong thing. It was safer in the kitchen.

Maybe not. A minute later I heard footsteps behind me as I took the brownies from the oven. I didn't need to turn my head to see who it was. The hairs on the back of my neck stood straight up.

"Sweetheart, it's so good your boyfriend is back in town. Now you can spend most of the holidays with him," Larissa said in her most syrupy voice. "And isn't it nice of Mrs. Langford to invite you along to their next trip?"

Sweetheart?

Before I could reply, Oliver joined us in the kitchen. He placed his hands over mine and took the hot baking tray from me, along with the oven mitts. "No, Maya's not going anywhere with that jerk. She stays here. This is her home as much as anyone else's." The tone of his voice invited no arguments.

My mouth dropped open. Oliver had never spoken to his mother like that. Shocked, my hand went to cover my mouth. What the hell was he doing? If he made a scene . . . oh God.

As if that wasn't enough, my father and Gerard appeared as well. Was there a memo about the dinner party being in the kitchen that I hadn't seen? Dad had his arm around Gerard's shoulder as if he was a long lost son or something to that effect, singing my domestic praises.

"Daddy, I've been baking these brownies since I started high school. Gerard's had a taste before," I said, irritation building in my gut.

"I've had her sweet cakes," Gerard said, a wicked grin on his face. "And all I can say is they're the sweetest I've ever tasted." Was he purposely riling Oliver while he had my father by his side? Payback for being chased of the house by my stepbrother? Years ago I would've high-fived him for a smart-ass comment like that. Now I was horrified as I watched Oliver's face turn red, a vein ticking in his tightly set jaw.

This was becoming a nightmare. Back in the dining room, my father allocated Gerard the seat next to mine. Not that Oliver ever sat beside me before, but it was just so damn obvious what my father was trying to do that it was actually embarrassing. Gerard, of course, gloated. For now, he had the upper hand and he knew it. He grinned at Oliver as if he had won the battle, his cockiness growing as my father kept making him feel like an important guest, commenting on how lucky I was to having such a "smart young man" as a boyfriend.

Oliver sat across from me with a stony expression, his eyes dark and stormy. His usual voracious appetite was apparently gone; he basically just scratched around his plate without really eating anything. I tried my best to avoid his gaze; all I could see were accusations and I really didn't need any extra crap on my plate. After the way he left me, broken and a mess, Oliver no longer had any right to tell me what to do.

A foot under the table rubbed up my leg. It took all of my self-control not to jump up. It was only when I finally gave in and took a peek at my stepbrother that I saw the corners of his mouth twist upwards. It wasn't Gerard trying to play footsie with me—he was too busy trying to sing his own praises to everyone who'd listen.

Oliver's eyes softened and he gave me a small smile that reached all the way to his eyes and crinkled the corners. It stole my breath away. For the first time, I saw his vulnerability.

In that moment everything stood still. It was only us in that room. Everything else was background noise—inconsequential. All that mattered to me were the eyes burning into mine with such intensity that it scorched my soul. My whole body tingled.

I felt deliciously alive. *Wanted*.

Even though he hadn't spoken a word.

There was no denying the way his eyes were undressing me, fucking me as they moved slowly down my body. I knew exactly what he was thinking just by the expression on his face and the fire in his eyes. If anyone else saw it, it would be game over.

Luckily for us, Gerard and his accomplishments were the topic of the moment. I couldn't care less. He could've been a billion dollar hedge fund baby with super powers and the mind of a rocket scientist and I wouldn't have seen him. I had eyes for one man only.

One man held my life in his hands.

One man could crush me with a look, set me alight with a smile.

One man I craved—my addiction out of control as always.

I wanted everyone to know about us. I wanted it out in the open. For Oliver to claim me publicly and make me his in the eyes of the world.

My heart ached, twisting and squeezing in my chest. The one thing I wanted the most in life, I could never have. I would never know what it feels like for everyone to know that I belonged to Oliver.

It was killing me inside as surely as if I'd stuck a fucking dagger into my own heart.

I loved him. Nothing wrong with loving my stepbrother.

Only it was far worse: I was *in love* with Oliver King.

Chapter 33
OLIVER

Did I believe in fighting for what I wanted?

Damn sure. But I also knew when to quit. When to give up the fight and leave. Here was a young man, admittedly a prick deluxe, but he could offer Maya the world I couldn't. It was time I saw this for what it really was—a sick obsession with my stepsister that could never go anywhere. It had no future.

Coming here tonight is a blessing and a curse.

It was in the moment I touched her leg and she looked up at me, her pain evident in her eyes, that my fucking heart flooded with so much love that I could've burst into flames. That was also the moment I knew I had to set her free—let her get on with her life.

Maya had so much promise; she was unassuming, beautiful, sexy, and smart. A great future ahead of her. She deserved the best. She deserved happiness. She deserved everything I couldn't give her.

Little bee owed me nothing. Nothing.

Not. One. Single. Thing.

I was the one who was blessed to have saved her life. The one who was lucky enough to find her and take her to be fixed. I used her vulnerability to get what I wanted. Forcing her to be mine with idle threats really meant that she wasn't mine at all. She was simply complying to save her father from further hurt. Maya was good like that, unlike some people who'd use others for their own gains. Like me. I was the monster she always said I was.

We were both damaged. The only difference? Mine was beyond repair. I'd never stop wanting her. Regardless of what happened, I'd always yearn to be near her. To hold her, to touch her, to fuck her.

That would never change until I drew my last fucking breath.

I fucking loved her.

Giving her one last smile, I pushed to my feet. "Please excuse me. I have some urgent business to get back to." I leaned over my mother and planted a kiss on her forehead. "Thanks for dinner, Mom. You really are a great cook, you know?"

Mom's eyes filled with tears as she looked up at me. I'd never paid her compliments since my father died. Indirectly I'd blamed her for what happened, when all this time he was the one who was fucked-up. Sick and depraved.

Just. Like. Me.

Mom must've known this was goodbye. Despite the way everyone treated her like a pretty but dumb blonde, Larissa was pretty smart. She'd let on that she was aware that there was something between Maya and I that we were trying to hide, but she didn't try to force me to tell her the details.

Maya sucked in a harsh breath. I didn't look at her. My resolve would crumble and instead of walking out, I'd beg her to have me—in front of everyone. I didn't care if they knew. I didn't care if they thought I was certifiable.

I only cared that she'd be happy. By setting her free, she could have an idyllic life with her boyfriend. I wanted that for her. The best life possible.

The joke was on me—I was the dumbest prick of all. How could I have imagined this would work? I thought I was smart buying a place in Santa Barbara. It fucking backfired all right. Now I was stuck with a place I didn't want to be anywhere close to. I'd rent it out, sell it, whatever—I really didn't care.

Without another word, my back stiff and unyielding, I left the room. I could feel Maya's eyes burn into me. Feel her sorrow even though I couldn't understand why she'd feel that after the way I'd treated her.

She'd soon be free.

As soon as I got to the door, I whipped my phone from my pocket and dialed the office. "Sofia, get me a one way ticket to Copenhagen. First flight available. And let Mr. Jensen know that I'll be at the office on Monday."

When I was offered a contract by a global IT company a few weeks ago, I had two choices: work from home anywhere in the world, or relocate to their head office in Denmark. With any luck, I'd be leaving soon.

"Yes, sir. No problem. Any time you prefer to fly?"

"Didn't you hear me, sweetheart? I said the first flight out. My bags are already packed," I snapped. "And get a taxi to pick me up in ten minutes. Oh, one more thing—I'm at my mother's house in Santa Barbara. Got that?"

"Oh. Okay."

I was already halfway up the stairs, my chest squeezing so tightly that I could hardly fucking breathe. My insides tumbled, bile pushing up my throat.

I had to do this. For my little bee. So she could carry on with her bright future. I'd fucked up and this was the only way to make it all right.

With long, determined strides I grabbed a suitcase and threw a few things into it. Who the fuck was I bluffing? I didn't care what I packed. The *one* thing I wanted to take had to stay behind. And with her, my heart would remain.

Gutted, I stormed down the stairwell, taking two steps at a time. My mother stood at the bottom, clutching her pearls. "Really, Oliver? You need to go this very minute?" Her skin was pale and her eyes wide.

And then my gaze fell on Maya. She stood behind my mother. It was the first time I'd seen them stand so close together, as if they needed one another's support. Her skin was ashen; she looked as if she'd faint any minute.

She should be glad I'm leaving. Happy I'm taking my sick, depraved needs to another continent. Instead tears were spilling down her beautiful face.

She's fucking crying?

Christ, I couldn't deal with that! If she'd cursed me or sent a snide remark my way like she always did, I'd walk away and never look the fuck back.

I stopped in front of her. "Maya. Little bee, please don't cry. It's crushing my fucking heart." I couldn't touch her without falling the fuck apart in front of everyone, so I just gripped my suitcase tighter, my knuckles white, and pulled the front door open.

The taxi stood there waiting. Good. I liked things to be organized and under control. I had to remember to give Sofia a raise. Funny the things that went through my mind while trying to pretend my fucking world hadn't just imploded.

Turned on its fucking axis.

I got into the taxi. "Airport," I barked. Fuck, even if I had to sleep on a chair until it was time to board, it would be better than staying at the house.

Sinking deep into the seat, my shoulders slumped forward. This was the hardest thing I'd done in my whole fucking life. I pressed my lips together and closed my eyes, pressing my fingers to my brows as my fucking heart broke into a trillion pieces.

Winter: Three years Later

Chapter 34
MAYA

I managed to disappoint my dad after all. At first he was devastated that I wasn't going to become a plastic surgeon like he was. I explained to him that working with people like Larissa who needed to keep updating their face to feel validated as a person wasn't for me.

And also, there was no way in hell I was working alongside Gerard. He was fast becoming Dad's protégé and the two of them spent hours discussing the intricacies of performing surgeries that would be undetected by the naked eye. More power to them, but that wasn't how I wanted to spend my life.

"Why would anyone want to be a clinical psychologist, working with depressed people who wander aimlessly through life?" My father's lips pursed together and I knew he was referring to my mother. Anger boiled up under my skin, threatening to burst out, but I managed to stay calm—until Gerard put in his two cents worth.

"People who hear voices and self-harm are the dregs of society. Shit, it would drive me nuts to work with people who felt the need to do that." The horror in his voice was unmistakable.

Uncontrollable rage filled my body at how these two seemingly intelligent men could be so judgmental without knowing anything about what it felt like. I understood how it felt to be unwanted. To be left behind, deserted by the people you depended on most.

Neither my father nor Gerard had ever seen the marks on my body. Never knew what I'd been through. Only two people knew about that. And he'd left my life without a proper goodbye or explanation.

The night Oliver had walked out and left me standing there, dumbfounded and questioning what I'd done to deserve him leaving me, again, was also the night I'd told Gerard, in front of both our families, that I was not his girlfriend and never would be.

"I'm focusing on my studies for the next few years. No distractions.

Definitely no boyfriends," I'd said, my world falling apart as I tried to keep my shit together.

The weird thing was that the person who supported me most was Larissa. She'd stepped forward and placed her arm around my shoulders. "Maya's right. She's so young; boys shouldn't be her priority right now."

I'd sucked in a breath, giving her a grateful smile. She nodded and smiled, but it didn't reach her eyes that brimmed with tears. Did she know about Oliver and me? She never said anything, not even after that night, yet I had a feeling she suspected something.

We were getting along much better lately, but my stepmom still wasn't on my go-to list of favorite people. Sometimes I'd find her in Oliver's bedroom, just staring at a picture of him or holding one of the t-shirts he'd left behind.

Shortly after he'd left me standing in the hallway, I'd gone upstairs to assess the damage. Most of his belongings were exactly where they'd always been. All that was missing was a family photo of all four of us at lunch last Thanksgiving. It was one of the few pictures that had both of us in it; the exact replica stood on a table in my bedroom. Every night before I went to sleep, I'd kiss my fingertips and place it on the glass over his face.

How I longed for that time. I'd give anything to turn back the clock and do things differently—I would've told my stepbrother how I felt about him. But I'd never gotten the chance, and now I never would.

*****

Larissa stood in the doorway of my bedroom, staring at me. The room was spinning and my vision had become blurry. "Oliver's hooked up with Bianca in Denmark?" I repeated to make sure I'd heard right.

That bitch still had her claws in my stepbrother. Images of them fucking the way they used to years ago made me feel sick to my stomach.

She nodded and came to stand next to the desk I was studying at for final exams. "He said he's thinking of asking her to marry him over Christmas." Her voice sounded a million miles away. I held on to my stomach and slouched forward—I was going to throw up all over Larissa's new shoes.

Stunned when my stepmother reached out and took hold of both of my shoulders, I looked up at her. "That bad, huh?" she said.

"What do you mean?" I was fighting to keep the contents of my stomach inside. My skin had gone ice cold and clammy, yet I felt a shiver run up my spine.

"You and Oliver."

"Larissa, don't play games with me. What are you suggesting?"

A smile tugged at her lips. "I've never seen my son love anyone as much as you. Including me or his father."

"Wh . . . what?" Bewildered, I searched her face for signs of mockery. There wasn't any.

"You're his little bee. He's been obsessed with you, Maya. And eventually, he grew to love you. Only I doubt either of you saw it coming."

"He . . . *what?*" Love was a strong word. No way in hell did Oliver King love me. It was impossible.

"You had no idea, did you? You were too busy fighting your own love for him."

How the hell had the woman who'd always been so self-possessed become so knowledgeable on my and her son's feelings. Usually she was so wrapped in her own little bubble that she was oblivious to the rest of the world.

"The two of you are drawn to one another like I was to Oliver's dad." She hesitated for a long moment before she continued. "He . . . he was my stepbrother too. Only, it didn't end well for us. Michael's death wasn't an accident. He committed suicide. He never really accepted that it was okay for us to be together."

Her eyes misted over and her voice sounded strained. She clutched her pearls the way she always did when she was distressed.

"I'm sorry. I never knew," I offered. I never had a clue what to say in situations like these. Sorry seemed so lame. But there it was, the best I could come up with.

Clearing her throat, she blinked her eyes fast before continuing. "He started drinking and sleeping around with younger girls. Much younger girls. Some barely legal . . . if that." Her cheeks had turned pink and her hands were trembling slightly. "I tried everything to make him love me again—tried to look young so he wouldn't fuck those little whores." The look of guilt and anguish on her face tugged at my heart. "Nothing worked. He drove his car straight into a tree, Maya. He killed himself because he couldn't deal with it."

I swallowed hard, blinking back my own tears. So this was why Oliver was so fucked up. Why he kept making remarks about being tainted that I couldn't understand. *It wasn't his fault.* None of it.

"Larissa, oh my God, nobody should have to go through that," I said, taking her hand in mine and leading her toward the bed so she could sit down. I sat beside her, squeezing her hand in mine.

"Alec . . . I met your father when I was at the lowest point in my life, the darkest nights of my existence, not trusting my own self worth because of my husband's behavior. Alec wasn't just my plastic surgeon, he also became my friend."

She smiled up at me, genuine adoration in her eyes when she spoke of my dad. "After we were married, Alec assured me I was beautiful and refused to do more work on me. I never believed him. I was getting older, things were getting saggy. So I went elsewhere to get my fix of botox and the knife. Of course he was aware of what was going on. I mean, the man is one of the best plastic surgeons in the country and I went to his colleagues for help. Ironic, huh? And being the stellar man that he is, Alec never said anything because he knew that I was still hurting inside. That I needed it. Only he wouldn't be the one doing it. Every time I got back from a visit to LA, I saw the hurt in his eyes, but I told myself that I was doing it for him."

I was proud of my dad for understanding her needs, but I still didn't like that she was hurting him. "Dad's good like that. He has a good heart."

"Yes, he is. When I lost Michael, we became even closer; both our spouses had left us by taking their own lives. Alec helped me more than I can ever tell you. Your father is a wonderful man."

I scrunched my nose up. "How did you pay for it all?"

"The stuff I had done in LA? I had some money from the insurances when Michael died. And Oliver. He gave me a loan from his inheritance from his grandparents. They were very wealthy. He got it all when he turned eighteen."

"Oliver's rich?" I gasped. He never flaunted it. Sure, he dressed well and had beautiful watches and a nice car, but he never bragged or flashed his wealth around.

Larissa nodded. "He's not a multimillionaire, but he's sitting on some pretty large stocks. He bought his own place in LA when he turned twenty, even though he was studying. Mostly he stayed away from here because he didn't know how to handle his feelings for you." There was no bitterness or anger in her voice; she was simply stating what she believed was a fact.

I shook my head, unable to absorb it all. "You and I have different recollections about my childhood then. As far back as I can remember, Oliver has hated me and made my life a living hell. And he had Bianca . . . and other women. It doesn't make sense."

Larissa laughed softly, her eyes sparkling with amusement. "For the same reason you baked brownies and bought new clothes whenever you knew he was coming. You were besotted by Oliver."

"Besotted? Hell no, I hated him. He was so mean to me."

She patted my hand reassuringly. "All a cover, my dear girl. Because he didn't want to go the same route his father had. He thinks Michael was weak. And in some ways he was. Michael refused to fight for us. He let everyone else's opinions matter more than us."

"Oliver knew?" I breathed. "About the two of you? That you were stepsiblings?"

She wrung her hands together. Her expression was pained. "Yes. It caused the biggest family scandal; people called us names, said we were living in sin, and that our child was from the devil himself. People are cruel,

Maya. They never consider what their words can do to another person."

I nodded. I'd seen it over and over again, and I hadn't been around that long. My heart ached for her, and especially for Oliver. He was just a boy. Why would people label him like that? No wonder he was so fucking angry all the time. I had no idea he'd been through shit like that. All that time I hated him for being mean to me, he was simply taking it out on me to hide his own grief.

"Oliver has been through a lot then. I think I'm finally starting to understand him better. Why he did some of the things—I wish he'd told me. I could have been his friend."

"He is way too stubborn for that. He didn't want to care for you, my dear." She shifted uncomfortably on the bed, casting her eyes to the floor.

"What?" I murmured, bracing myself.

"I was so ashamed when Oliver found out that his father slept with girls his own age. Subconsciously, I think maybe I thought I could have stopped that from happening. If I looked younger, or prettier, his father wouldn't have strayed. Ultimately wouldn't have wrapped himself around a damn tree."

I grabbed hold of Larissa and pulled her closer, hugging her as she sobbed.

"It's not your fault, Larissa. You were dealt a cruel hand," I said. I was beginning to understand Larissa a lot better—why she was so damn obsessed with how she looked to the point of absurdness. She was hiding her insecurity behind her looks. I couldn't help pitying her a little. Because my father was right; she was a beautiful woman in her own right. She didn't need all the surgery she'd become addicted to.

"Thanks. I try to remind myself of that. I just don't want Alec to go the same way. And I want you and Oliver to be happy."

I sucked in a breath. "So you didn't hate me, then?"

"God, no. The reason I wanted you out of the house isn't what you think; I wanted you to fall in love with someone else. But it was too late. There was already something between you and my son. I never wanted either of you to go through what I had. It ate me alive. People's nastiness and bullying can destroy lives. Throwaway comments can cause suicide. That's why I think what you're studying is so helpful to others and why I support you."

Larissa reached out and took hold of both my hands, pushing my shirtsleeves up. Her thumbs caressed softly over my wrists. "I've known about these for a long time. Although the scars have healed on your skin, the scars in your heart are still there, haunting you."

My gaze met hers. For the first time we really connected.

"Does Daddy know?" I held my breath, waiting for her answer.

"Yes," she whispered. "Oliver told us after it happened. He was beside himself."

What?

My mouth hung slightly open as I tried to absorb it. Oliver told them and then blackmailed me into sex with him for the very thing he'd already disclosed? Why would he do that? It didn't make sense.

"He never said he'd told you. He said it was or secret." I couldn't keep the disbelief out of my voice.

"He made us promise to watch you all the time. That's when your father installed security cameras around the house. It was all Oliver's idea. He was terrified you'd try it again and that he wouldn't be there to find you."

"Daddy . . . you . . . if you knew, why didn't anyone say anything?"

Her hands smoothed over her skirt. "Oliver was convinced he could help you. That's when he decided to move back to Santa Barbara, even though he'd said he hated the place. He wanted to be closer to you. Of course he didn't tell your father that. But I understood what was going on."

With my fist I rubbed large circles over my heart to ease the ache that settled there. "What should I do, Larissa? Help me, please. I love Oliver so fucking much it hurts."

Her eyes widened. "Oh dear, I never thought you'd admit that. That's the first step." She paused, tilting her head to look at me for a long moment. "What do you want, Maya? How do you want your life to be?"

I didn't hesitate for a second. "With Oliver. Wherever he is. However he is. Just as long as I'm with him, that's all that matters. He can't marry Bianca. It has to be me. I love him with all my heart and soul."

"Oliver's little bee." She smiled. "Those are strong words. Your love will be tested. There will be people who know your history and will look down on you. I never knew when I agreed to marry your father that it could affect you and my son like this—I didn't think he'd fall for you the way he has. He always went for blondes, like Bianca. I thought you were safe."

Her words rattled me. My head was spinning with all the new information I'd just learned. Sometimes nothing was as it seemed. Our reality was so different than what we showed the outside world.

"It's not your fault, Larissa. None of it. Not what happened to Michael, or me, or Oliver. Now that you've told me, I understand you so much better. I get where your insecurity comes from—and I don't blame you at all."

"Thank you," she breathed, her eyes misty.

It still didn't solve my problem with Oliver. How could I stop him from making the biggest mistake of his damn life?

"Go to Oliver. Talk to him," she said as if she had read my mind.

"Go to Denmark? I—I can't. What if Bianca is there? What if Oliver rejects me?"

Larissa cocked her head, a small smile twisting the corners of her lips.

"How much do you love my son, Maya? Is he worth fighting for?"

I nodded, tears streaming down my cheeks. I swallowed the burning lump in my throat. "I love him so much. I just had a hard time admitting it. I've tried everything to resist it, but I just can't shake him. I'd give my life for that man."

Larissa rose to her feet. "I'll make the arrangements. Bring him back home, Maya. He belongs here with us. We can finally be a real family."

I blinked fast. Larissa was helping me?

How things had changed.

Chapter 315
OLIVER

Although I'd been in Denmark for three years now, I hated the freezing cold of December. Back in California it was cold, but it never cut through into my bones like it did here.

I stood by the window and watched the snowflakes flutter to the ground. My insides felt as cold as those ice droplets. I was supposed to be excited. I'd picked a ring and made dinner arrangements. I was finally moving on with my life. At twenty-five, I wanted kids of my own, and there really wasn't any point in waiting to get married any longer. Bianca could satisfy my needs enough that I would be okay.

"There's someone here to see you, Mr. King." My secretary said in her thick Scandinavian accent. She stood in the doorway waiting for my reply, looking rather apprehensive. "She won't give me her name."

"I don't have time now. Tell her to make an appointment and come back another day. And get her name." Dismissing her, I went back to my computer. I had deadlines looming and more to do than I had hours in a day.

Work soothed my soul, kept my mind from wandering to places I wanted to avoid. The more I worked, the less I had time to think about Maya and what I was planning to ask Bianca. Because if I was honest, I'd felt uneasy and restless since I'd decided to take the plunge.

Maybe I'd feel better after I'd asked her and she agreed. It was probably normal to feel this way. How would I know any different? Yet I couldn't help being a bit disappointed that I wasn't more excited. I always imagined I'd feel elated when I popped the question. It was a big fucking moment in anyone's life.

"I'm afraid I can't come back another day. I need to see you today, Oliver." My head jerked up when I recognized the American accent. Was I fucking hallucinating? Lately I'd been waking up in a cold sweat—always dreaming of Maya. Putting a continent between us hadn't changed anything, and I couldn't escape her in my dreams. And now I was hearing her fucking voice when I was awake.

My mouth fell open as I stared over Mrs. Olsen's shoulder. Was I dreaming? Maya stood there in a cream colored coat and a red scarf around her neck. Her pitch black hair tumbled over her shoulders and down her back. Her cheeks were flushed and her sweet lips were pulled into a small smile.

She was even more fucking beautiful than I remembered. An apparition.

I pushed to my feet, my legs shaky. I'd wake up from this dream at any moment.

"Maya," I said, barely able to get the word out. I waved to Mrs. Olsen to leave us alone. She smiled at us and pulled the door closed behind her. She never did that when Bianca came to my office—in fact, she made a point of disrupting our conversations so frequently that I sometimes felt like scolding her.

"I'm surprised you remember my name. I haven't heard from you in three years, brother."

I scowled. I *hated* that fucking word—it had ruined both my parent's lives and mine.

"What are you doing here, Maya? Why are you in Denmark?" She was turning my whole fucking perfectly organized world upside down again. Just when I thought everything was under fucking control.

"Do I need a reason?" Her eyebrow lifted and she pursed her lips the way she always had when she was exasperated. Fuck, how I'd missed that.

"No . . . I—"

She threw back her head and laughed. "I have a few reasons, actually. One of them is research. I thought you could help me with that."

"Help you? *How?*" I swallowed hard. Why was it so hot in this fucking office? I needed air.

"I'm doing a research paper for my thesis on step siblings. Since you're pretty much an expert on that topic, I thought I could interview you."

She's not here for me. "Oh? That's it? That's why you're here?" I couldn't keep the disappointment out of my voice.

What did you expect, Oliver? You were the asshole who'd left.

She unwrapped the scarf from around her neck and placed it over the back of the chair. I watched as she pulled at each finger of her gloves before removing them from her hands. Slowly, she unbuttoned her coat. I drank each movement in, totally enthralled by such a simple everyday action. But there was just something in the way she moved that captivated me.

"No, there's more. Much more. But that can wait until we catch up on one another's news." This woman in front of me was Maya, yet she was somehow different. Self-confidence oozed from her like I'd never seen. It was attractive as fuck.

Don't go there. Don't let your dirty thoughts sully this. It's not what you hope it is.

Nothing had changed about how she made me feel. As soon as the deep dimples appeared in her cheeks, my cock stiffened. Jesus fuck. She removed the coat, laying it over the back of the chair next to her scarf. She wore a deep crimson dress, hugging every curve of her perfect body. She was clearly no longer a teenager, and had morphed into a full-bodied woman. The deep V cut in the front of her dress drew my eyes directly to her ample cleavage.

Just when I thought I'd finally worked her out of my fucking system, here she was, taunting me with the body and face that haunted my dreams. "Eyes up here, Oliver," she said, reminding me of her words at the pool all those years ago.

My gaze shifted slowly, and somewhat reluctantly, up her body to her eyes. I sucked in a harsh breath. Those green orbs were dancing with delight, sucking me into their depths. I couldn't tear my fucking eyes away.

I held on to the back of my chair, partly to compose myself, partly to hide the fact that my dick had gone rock solid. Fuck.

"Undressing me with your eyes, Oliver?" she said, laughing softly. Fuck, if I thought the eighteen-year-old Maya was dangerous, her adult version was completely mesmerizing. Electricity crackled in the air, causing every cell in my body to come alive and be on high alert.

I wanted to touch her. Feel those soft curves press into me. Kiss those fucking lips. Instead I stood frozen as if I'd seen an apparition.

The door cracked open, and in stepped my soon-to-be fiancé, looking smoking hot in tight leather pants and boots. But the attraction I felt for her could never be as magnetic as the pull toward Maya. Gravity had taken hold of my heart and I was powerless to change it.

Bianca was going to be my wife soon. *Pull your shit together, King.*

The smile on Bianca's face slid right off when she saw my stepsister standing in the middle of my office. She pulled her nose up as if she smelled something off. "Maya? What brings you to Denmark?" Bianca's eyes were wide, her tone hostile. It was impossible to miss her disdain.

Before Maya could answer I cut in, suddenly finding my tongue. "She's here for work."

Bianca walked over to me and grabbed hold of my tie, aggressively pulling me toward her. "I missed you, baby," she said, hooking one leg around my thigh and rubbing her pussy unashamedly against me. "I thought I'd come to the office early so we could make out before we went to dinner. You know how that stimulates your appetite," she said, winking at me.

Suddenly the red lipstick she wore with her too-brassy blonde hair made her look too much like a whore to carry my babies. Uneasiness settled in the pit of my stomach at the thought of waking to her face every day for the rest of my fucking life. The collar of my shirt strangled me, making me hot and uncomfortable.

Laughing, I pulled away and unbuttoned the top of my shirt. I loosened my tie and pulled it off. I hated these fucking things, but I'd had to wear it to a meeting earlier.

My gaze crossed back to Maya. She stood there, biting hard into her bottom lip the way she always did when she doubted herself. Seeing her vulnerability made my heart squeeze painfully.

"Plans have changed. We are going for a drink before dinner and Maya is coming with us," I said matter-of-factly, as if this was completely normal.

The look on Bianca's face was priceless. She never liked Maya and still referred to her as the kid whenever she asked me about my family back home, even though she knew perfectly well that Maya had just turned twenty-one.

Bianca watched through narrowed eyes as Maya dressed back into her coat and scarf. She held both gloves in her hand and nodded when I asked if she was ready.

Awkwardness had settled in the thick air between the three of us.

As we stepped into the elevator, Bianca gunned for pole position, ensuring she stood between Maya and I. Twirling her hair between her fingers, Bianca trained her eyes on the descending numbers above the door. Why did people always do that? Suddenly it irked me beyond belief.

Maya had turned her head down, affording me the chance to openly stare at her face. Drinking in the sight of the vision before me, I noticed that Maya's cheeks were a little fuller than I remembered, and those bee sting lips—fuck, they were sensational. She had them coated in some glittery shit that made them look even more delicious.

The doors opened and we stepped outside. The cold air hit me between the eyes, but it was better than the stifling air back in my office.

Mrs. Olsen had called for a cab, and it stood idling in the specially marked taxi area. At the last minute, I decided to let both women sit in the back as I slid into the front seat next to the driver. I didn't want the first time I touched Maya after all this time to be when we were sandwiched into the back of a taxi.

"Awww, babe, I wanted to cuddle with you," Bianca whined.

One thing I was sure of—I was still an asshole. But letting the two women sit in the back together gave me a few moments to clear my fucking head. It was pounding with a motherfucker of a headache, and I knew exactly why. As Maya had bent down to get into the back seat, her scent had wafted to my nostrils and hit me straight in the dick. Some things never changed. I closed my eyes and massaged my temples with the pads of my thumbs.

Fuck.

We stopped in front of a trendy bar ten minutes later. I hopped out of the car to open the door for Maya, who'd sat behind me. She avoided my gaze, but her cheeks burned red, reminding me of the slinky dress she wore under her coat. I wanted to take it off her fucking body with my teeth and ravish her. Instead I stood like a statue, holding the door open like an idiot.

Seconds later, Bianca came barreling around the front of the taxi and bumped into Maya, knocking her purse out of her hand. The contents scattered over the sidewalk, sending a look of panic over Maya's face.

Cursing at Bianca under my breath, I bent over to pick up the items that had fallen out. My gaze narrowed in on a blue box tied up with a ribbon that seemed vaguely familiar. Drawn to it, I picked it up, memories of it streaming into my consciousness. It was the box that always sat on my mother's vanity.

"Maya?" I said, watching her expression for clues as I held it out to her.

She shrugged. "Keep it. Larissa sent it. She said you may want to use it."

A conversation with my mom—a happier time from my childhood—played out in my mind. *"Oliver, one day you'll inherit these rings when you're grown up. They're my mother's engagement and wedding rings, and she wanted you to have them. She left you a message inside the box, so be sure to read it before you give these rings to anyone, okay?"*

Could this be the same box? I stuck it into my coat pocket before Bianca's curiosity forced me to open it. I wanted to be completely alone when I read the message that was written in my grandmother's beautiful slanted handwriting. I'd read it when I was a kid, but it didn't really make all that much sense to me. I hoped that I'd understand it better now.

I thought I had my fucking life under control. Turned out to be the biggest lie I'd ever told myself.

Chapter 36
MAYA

What if Larissa was completely wrong? What if Oliver had moved on and really wanted to marry his longtime fuck buddy? I couldn't bring myself to think of her any other way, yet jealousy gripped my heart as I sat there wishing I could be her.

Since I'd walked into his office, my stepbrother hadn't attempted to touch me in any way—not even a brotherly hug. Instead it felt like he was ensuring Bianca was always between us, like now, sitting at the counter. She was all over him, her hand on his leg.

Sometimes they'd slip into talking Danish to one another; it came so naturally to them. Oliver was smart, so I wasn't surprised when I heard him order our drinks from the barman in fluent Danish. But talking to her and excluding me from their conversation hurt like a motherfucker.

"Um, I need to go to the ladies room," I said, sliding off the barstool and back onto the impossibly high heels I'd worn to make my legs look longer. I should have saved myself the effort of dressing to kill. The dress, the shoes, the hair, the makeup—none of it made any damn difference. Suddenly I just wanted to go home, curl up in bed, pull the covers over my head, and go into a deep sleep.

Bianca slipped off her chair and hooked into my arm. "I need to go too. We'll go together, yeah?" She leaned over and kissed Oliver full on the mouth, sticking her tongue down his throat. I rolled my eyes. For fuck sake, she was going to be gone ten minutes tops; she wasn't leaving the country. Jealousy did nasty things to me, and right now I wished I had a voodoo doll of Bianca I could stick all sorts of pins into.

Oliver grinned sheepishly and took a large sip of his beer. I followed Bianca as she dragged me through the crowd of trendy hipsters. A few times I had to grab hold of something to stop me from twisting my ankle in the precarious heels I was wearing, yet she never slowed down. Only when we reached the inside of the washroom did she let go of my arm.

She swung around, glaring at me with unadulterated hatred in her eyes. "Listen kid, I don't know what your fucking game is, but Oliver's mine. He has been for years. We would've been married a long time ago if you hadn't fucked with his head." She threw back her head and laughed. "Yeah, bitch, I know all about you seducing your brother. You're such a slut. I'm surprised he didn't throw you right out when you came to his office." Pure venom dripped from her voice.

Staggering backward as if she'd slapped me, my hand moved to cover my mouth.

"That's right, bitch, you should be ashamed of yourself. Oliver doesn't want you—he told me himself. He said moving here was the best thing he could've done. So spare yourself further embarrassment and just leave before it gets ugly."

My throat burned as I bit back the tears. God, I was a fool for believing Oliver would want me. Of course he didn't— he wouldn't have move to another damn continent if he did. Heat flushed over my cheeks as the truth dawned on me. Bianca was right—Oliver hadn't even attempted to touch me, and he looked anywhere but at me.

Did Larissa purposely lie to me so that I could make a complete idiot of myself while she laughed at me behind my back? And if Bianca knew everything about Oliver and me, he must've told her. They probably laughed at my stupidity, too. I'd felt so confident in myself coming here, and now I just felt unwanted and plain stupid.

"Um . . . I have a headache. Please tell Oliver I said goodbye," I said as calmly as I could. I couldn't get out of this place fast enough.

"Shall I tell him an emergency came up and you had to go back home?" she offered, grinning.

Tears blurred my vision and any second they were going to fall hard and fast. I didn't need her to see that, too—it'd just give her and Oliver something else to laugh about.

"Tell him anything you damn well want." I spun around on my heels and made my way to the exit, escaping into the cold night air without my coat or scarf. Thankfully I'd taken my purse to freshen my lip gloss and didn't need to face Oliver again to retrieve it. I didn't care that the icy wind whipped around my body; I just wanted to put as much distance between us as I could.

Larissa had a fucking lot of explaining to do. But it was my own fault. I'd wanted to believe her. Wanted to think that after three years Oliver yearned for me as much as I did for him. That he felt as incomplete without me as I felt without him.

But now I knew the truth. He probably hadn't thought of me for a day since he left the US. He probably came to Denmark because Bianca was there. What a stupid fool I was. When it came to Oliver, I just couldn't ever see the damn truth, even if it hit me over the head with a stick.

I flagged down the first taxi that looked unoccupied. Luckily the driver understood English and I gave him the address of the hotel I'd booked into only hours earlier. I'd get some sleep—probably cry all night, of course—and then after breakfast I'd figure out what to do next.

At this moment it was just all too damn hard. I didn't want to think, didn't want to feel. All the insecurities of feeling lost and alone, unwanted and unloved, came flooding back.

I couldn't wait to get back to my hotel room, away from prying eyes. A woman in a low-cut, clingy red dress without a coat to shield her from the weather probably screamed *slut*.

The taxi driver grinned from ear to ear. I didn't want to wait for change, so he'd just scored a huge tip. I practically ran to the elevator, praying it would swallow me up and take me up into the sky where I'd be safe.

Fumbling in my purse for my magnetic key card, I cursed as I remembered I'd been so excited when I left the hotel earlier that I'd just shoved it into my coat pocket. But luck was on my side that night after all. The cleaner for our floor was just wheeling her trolley laden with dirty sheets toward the elevator when I called out to her.

"Hi," I said with a wide smile as I approached her. God, I hoped she still remembered me from earlier—it would be so much easier than going back to reception for a new key. "I'm wondering if you can help me get back into my room? I accidentally left my coat behind and my key is in the pocket." I rubbed up and down my arms, still feeling the cold from earlier despite the warmth of the hotel.

She looked up and smiled back, "I don't normally do this, but since I was here when you checked in and asked for an allergy-free pillow, I remember your lovely face."

Thank goodness Daddy taught me to tip well—I was sure that helped her remember me. Wearily she shuffled back to my door and opened it with her master key card, letting me into the darkness.

"Thanks, that's very kind of you. Saves me an elevator trip to the lobby."

"Goodnight. Hope you can get your coat back tomorrow."

"Yeah, me too," I lied. I closed the door and switched on the lights before I made my way straight into the bathroom to scratch through my toiletries. My blades had to be there somewhere. I always carried a packet with me wherever I went. Pure stainless steel. No expiration date.

I'd made up my mind on the short taxi ride to the hotel. Maybe it was brain freeze from the cold, but I'd made a monumental decision. This was the night I was putting an end to all the bullshit that was my fucking life. I'd had enough of it all. It ended right there, right at that moment.

In a hotel room in Denmark. All alone.

Chapter 37
OLIVER

Watching Bianca swing her hips as she sauntered back toward me, I kept looking behind her, waiting for Maya to appear. When she finally reached the table I'd secured for us, my stepsister still hadn't appeared. Worried that she'd gotten lost since I'd moved a few feet away from where we'd sat before, my eyes kept darting around the space searching for her.

"Darling, the kid had to go back to her hotel. She has a headache. She said for me to tell you goodbye and that we should enjoy our evening together." She smiled at me, flicking her fringe backward.

"What the fuck, Bianca. What if she gets lost? And she doesn't have her fucking coat either." I glared at her, unable to comprehend her stupidity. Through gritted teeth, I hissed, "And *never* call Maya *the kid* again, understand?"

That was all I had time for. I had to find Maya before she disappeared. I grabbed a few notes from my wallet and threw them onto the table. "Get a taxi back to your place. I'm going to find Maya."

Thank fuck I hadn't allowed Bianca to move into my place. Sure, she slowly brought stuff over and left it at my place, but I made a point of not letting her feel as if it were her home.

Snatching up Maya's coat and scarf, I went in the direction of the bathroom, hoping to bump into her before she left the building. It was fucking freezing out there and I didn't want her catching her death.

I pushed my way impatiently through the throngs of people who'd multiplied like locusts in the last half hour, my eyes frantically searching for a dark head. A few times I thought I'd spotted her, but every time I was disappointed when it wasn't her. My gut dropped to my shoes and my mouth went dryer by the second.

Maya was gone. Fuck.

My stomach pulled into a tight knot when I realized I had no idea where she was staying or what her phone number was. A few months back I'd caved in and called her number, just to hear her voice on her mailbox, and I'd discovered that she'd discontinued that service.

Her coat hung over my arm, and I could smell her fragrance lingering on it. It was driving me insane. But then a thought hit me—I checked the pockets, grinning when I saw a keycard for a hotel that was about five minutes away.

"Find me a taxi," I yelled above the noise to the young waiter as I shoved money into his hand. He nodded and scurried off while I glanced around the room again. Still nothing.

Two minutes later the dude signaled me that a taxi was waiting. They must've been lined up outside the place, and for once I was glad I could escape the jolly bustle of a Friday night. The fact that Bianca let Maya leave without her coat was pissing me off more and more. I clenched my jaw, anger swirling in my gut. Jealousy was an ugly look on anyone. I knew because I'd worn it more times than I cared to admit.

I shivered as I opened the door to slide in beside the driver. I wanted to be up at the front so I could look out for a Maya—if she hadn't taken a taxi, she'd be frozen stiff. Directing the taxi driver to the hotel, I sat forward in my seat, my gaze pinned to the road.

Being a Friday night, there was a hell of a lot more traffic in this part of town than midweek. I cursed as we stopped at one traffic light after another, sometimes barely moving a few yards before stopping again. As soon as we turned off the busy road though, I instructed the driver to go as fast as he could. I couldn't wait any longer to find Maya.

I'd been checking the meter as we drove, so I just pulled a fifty from my wallet and threw it down onto the seat as soon as I'd hopped out.

"Thanks—and keep the change," I said to the driver as I closed the door and marched into the hotel foyer through the revolving doors. I checked the magnetic card for a room number. Fuck. Nothing.

The line at the desk was longer than I had the patience for. For some bizarre reason I had the strangest sensation that I had to hurry or I'd be too late. For what I didn't know, but I'd had a sort of sixth sense when it came to Maya, and I knew something was going to happen.

A pretty redhead dressed in the hotel uniform stood alone on the far side of the desk, her attention on a computer. I was in luck. Plastering my most charming smile on my face, I walked over to where she stood. I cleared my throat so she would look up at me.

A small frown marred her forehead as she moved her head upwards, irritation just under the false smile she was about to present me with. "Good evening," I said in my strongest American accent. Danish women were suckers for the way I spoke. The frown evaporated and was replaced with a genuine smile.

"Good evening, sir. How may I be of assistance?" The way she was checking me out, I was sure she had a few things in mind, but I didn't have time for small talk. Time was ticking and I had to get to that room. But I also knew that if I didn't play along, she could give me grief—I turned the charm factor up a notch.

"I was wondering if you could help me, sweetheart? I need the room number to this key card please."

Her eyebrow shot up as she took the card from me. "We don't give out room numbers unless we have the occupant's name on record," she said in a heavy accent.

Not wanting to piss her off, I leaned against the counter casually. "My sister left her coat in the taxi." I held up the coat as proof. "Poor thing, she must be jetlagged." That part at least was true.

"I'm just about to sign off for the night, and then I'm out of here," she said, smiling widely. "If you want, I could arrange for someone to take the coat up to her and you could buy me a drink to say thank you."

Fuck. This wasn't going my way. "That's the best offer I've had all night, beautiful. But little sis left her asthma inhaler in the pocket and I just want to make sure she's okay." I was completely fucked if she asked to see the damn inhaler I'd just fabricated.

Alarm came over her face. "Oh, my little brother has asthma, too. It's terrible having to watch him suffer sometimes. His seems to get worse at night." I wouldn't have a clue, so I was willing to go along with anything she said if it would get me to Maya.

She turned her attention back to the computer and typed something into it. "Tell you what. Go check on your sister, and when you're done I'll be here." She wrote something on a piece of paper and handed it to me together with the key card.

"Thanks, babe," I said, relief washing over me.

She laughed. "Sure. Your sister is in room 3003 on the top floor. Now hurry; I'm waiting for that drink."

Crossing the foyer with long strides, I pressed the button to the elevator. If she'd just told me the room number, what had she written on the paper? I opened it slowly.

Clara—room 515. I'll be waiting.

Underneath she'd scribbled a heart and a smiley face. Crumpling the paper into a ball, I shoved it into my pocket as the doors opened. I stepped inside and sent up a prayer of gratitude that there weren't ten other people in the car all wanting to get off at a different floor. As I went to press the button for the thirtieth floor I heard a laugh. Clara was inside the car with me.

What the fuck just happened?

Clara inserted a card into a slot and pressed a code into the keypad.

"I thought I'd come with you to check on your sister." She waved her card at me, smiling. "This means we go directly to the top floor with no stops. Handy, huh?"

Fuck, how was I going to get rid of her? I had to keep my shit together. "That's cool sweetheart, but why don't you go to your room, five-one-five, and I'll see you in a bit?" Luckily I'd remembered the number so that I'd sound more convincing.

"And miss all the fun?" she said, laughing as she pulled the front zipper of her dress down all the way to her waist. She wasn't wearing a bra. "I love fucking in the elevator, American," she said as she pushed the dress off her shoulders and let it drop to the floor. Fuck me—she wasn't wearing panties either. She'd looked so professional, innocent even, standing behind the desk earlier.

I groaned loudly. Her legs went on forever in black heels and her pussy had been trimmed with only a small landing strip of dark brown hair. The red hair was fake.

Large brown nipples scraped against my arm. "Let's see how quickly you can come." Seconds later her hand was on my dick, stroking through the fabric. I felt myself harden under her skillful fingers. A day ago I would have been up for this. A quick fuck on the way to the top floor was nearly as good as the mile high club. I wasn't unfamiliar with down and dirty stranger sex. No names. No emotions. Just raw fucking.

She tugged on my pants zipper and pulled it down expertly—she'd obviously had plenty of practice. Stunned, I watched her hand disappear into the opening and grab hold of my cock while she licked her lips.

Gripping both her wrists with one hand, I pushed her backwards. "Babe, I want to fuck you all night long, not just here." I grabbed hold of a nipple and twisted until she gasped. "And I'm the one who calls the shots," I growled, squeezing her tit forcefully in my palm, intending pain. "Do you understand?"

She nodded. I turned her around and smacked her ass hard. She yelped, so I smacked again. "Later baby, when I can give you my full attention. Now get dressed like a good girl and go wait for me in your room."

"Oh God," she panted. "I'm so fucking wet. Just fuck me now and then I'll go wait for you."

"Did I say you can talk?" I growled, lifting my hand for another smack.

She whimpered as my hand connected to her ass, her pussy juices dripping down her leg. I threw back my head and laughed like a madman. Yesterday I would have fucked her upside down if that was what she wanted. Now I wanted no part of her. I had another woman on my mind.

Maya. She was *all* that mattered.

The elevator came to a stop.

"Get dressed," I said as I left, already forgetting about her as I scrutinized the numbers looking for Maya's room. She'd better be there. She'd better be okay. I slapped my hand to my forehead. I was the dumbest fuck on earth. No other pussy—no other woman could come close to Maya. I'd always known that. I wasn't going to lose her again. To anyone or anything.

Once I reached her door I froze. My heart hammered against my ribs and my mouth went dry. I couldn't just barge in even though I had a key. I knocked on the door and took a step back, controlling my breathing in an effort to stay the fuck calm.

A minute later I knocked again. Maybe she was asleep already. Jetlag was a real thing. I knocked again, this time considerably louder. Still nothing.

Visions of her on a crimson bathroom floor, blood trickling from her veins, flashed through my mind. My heartbeat sped up and my chest tightened so that I could hardly breathe.

Fuck me, I was going in.

Swiping the white piece of plastic with trembling hands, I heard the beep and then a green light flashed. I was in! I turned the knob and pushed the door open slowly. I didn't want to scare her if she was sleeping, but I also didn't want to take my sweet-ass time.

I stumbled into the darkness, stretching my arms out in front of me so that I wouldn't bump into anything.

"Maya? Are you here?" My voice echoed around the room, unanswered. I reached for a bed lamp. I needed light so I could see what the fuck was going on. Fear had gripped my insides as silence swirled around me.

Her perfume permeated my nostrils—she'd been in this room only a short while ago. The light flickered to life a few seconds later. My gaze fell on the empty bed. It hadn't been slept in at all. Fuck, no! *Please don't let my little bee be lying on the bathroom floor.*

I'd never really prayed before, but now I was on speed dial to heaven. The light from the lamp was too dim to see into the bathroom. Why did they make these rooms so fucking dark? And cold. A shiver ran down my spine; I was chilled to the fucking bone.

"Maya? For fuck sake, answer me!" This wasn't the way I planned on greeting her when I came looking for her, but right at this moment it was all I could muster not to scream her name into the darkness. Fumbling, I found a light switch and flicked it on, feeling relief when a light blinked to life. Preparing myself for the worst, I couldn't help sucking in extra oxygen as I stared at the bathroom floor.

Empty.

No Maya.

Where the fuck was she?

Chapter 38
MAYA

As soon as I closed the door to my hotel room, I went to the bathroom to find my trusty blades. They were always there. Waiting for me. No judgment. No pity. Cold and hard and real.

I hadn't needed them in a long time, and I should have thrown them out a long time ago, but like an alcoholic always craving the next drink, I wanted to know I had access to my source of relief at any time I needed it.

Was it sick that while I was studying to help other people overcome their own problems I myself had a set of special blades stashed away in case? *In case of what? Life sucked?* Yeah, sometimes life hurt, sometimes it wasn't fair. Sometimes we didn't understand why something was happening to us.

But it was just life. *Normal life.*

And hurting was part of living as much as what happiness and joy were.

I wish I could tell that to Megan Childs. My mom didn't have to do it, and neither did I. There was far more to live for.

Life, in spite of sometimes being fucked up, was beautiful.

It was time to take the blades out of their special case. Slowly unwrapping the surgical steel razors, I hummed softly to myself. The blades glistened in the mirror as the light reflected off them, catching my attention and causing me look up into the mirror.

I appraised my own face as if I'd just seen it for the first time.

Astonished, I kept staring into my eyes, dulled by the intense pain in their depths. They appeared flat and dead.

Yet it wasn't the same face staring back at me as always. This woman was different. Stronger. She knew what she wanted out of life, and it wasn't to hurt anyone or anything she loved. Including herself.

Although the pain that came from loving someone so hard and being rejected was impossible to ignore, this wasn't the way my life had to play out. I could choose another course. I could keep living and finding joy in other things. I could focus on my job and help other damaged souls. I had a purpose and a place in this world, even if it was without the love of my life.

Yes, Oliver had become that for me. Nobody else would do. Even when we were apart, thoughts of him consumed me. That would never change, but I could live with it. I was capable of dealing with the agony of unrequited love.

My heart was shredded—cut into a million pieces. No blade was responsible. All it took was one man not wanting me like I wanted him.

Maybe time would heal it? Dull the constant ache? Nothing could compare to how shattered I was. Losing Oliver was worse than losing my life. No amount of hurting or harming outwardly could come close to the suffering of my heart.

I placed the blade back in its wrapping and walked to the bin. I didn't need these any longer. There's no point. Those sharp edges could never cut as deep as Bianca's words had.

With a wry smile, I uncurled my fingers and let go, dropping the metal pieces into the garbage where they belonged. The feeling of elation that flowed through me surpassed the despair I'd felt earlier.

Proud as fuck of myself, I rushed to pack my bags. *I'd live.* I'd soak up whatever life had to offer. But right this minute, I had to get as far away as possible from the cause of my bleeding heart.

Five minutes later I made my way down the elevator towards the checkout desk. "Hi," I said as brightly as I could muster to the woman behind the desk who'd booked me in a short few hours ago. "I have an emergency to tend to. I need to leave and get to the airport as soon as possible. Can I please settle my account and have a taxi pick me up?"

"Sure, Miss Childs. You're lucky you caught me—I'm just about to go off duty. I'll quickly finalize your account before I go." She smiled up at me, her eyes running over my body. "By the way, I love your leather jacket. Very trendy."

"Thanks." The jacket was nowhere near warm enough without my coat, but it would have to do until I could get home.

"Taxis are waiting outside. Since it's a Friday night, most of our patrons go out to the popular bars around this area. Pity you couldn't stay to enjoy Danish hospitality."

"Yeah, pity," I echoed, impatient to get the hell out of there. She didn't need to know that the short while I spent at one of the lovely trendy bars in this city was one of the worst experiences of my life."

Sliding into the back seat of the taxi, I sighed deeply.

"Where to, lady?"

"Airport please," I said, fighting to hold back the tears. I'd come with so much hope in my heart. All my dreams had been dashed and I just wanted to get out of there.

Where to, lady? The driver's question echoed in my mind. Where was I going?

I closed my eyes and let my mind run free. If I could be anywhere in the world right now, where would I want to be? Heck, I'd already flown all the way to Europe; a short flight to somewhere I'd always dreamed of going would be a perfect time-out to heal my broken heart.

London. I'd always wanted to see the place my mother was born and raised before meeting my father and moving to California. It always lurked somewhere in the back of my mind that maybe one of the reasons she felt so blue when I was born was that she was so far away from her family. Maybe I could look up an aunt or a cousin and get to know my mother a bit better through their eyes. I'd never had real contact with them besides a few birthday cards and Christmas gifts. I smiled. Between Google and my great research skills, I'd be able to trace somebody down.

"Thanks," I said to the driver as I reached for my purse to pay the fair. He handed my bags to me.

"Hope you find your happiness, Miss." He said with a wide, gap-toothed grin. *Was it that obvious?*

"I hope so, too," I said, smiling and adding an extra tip to the fare.

At the counter, I managed to purchase a ticket to a flight that was boarding in just over an hour. Great. I'd have time to browse the news agency and grab a paperback to read. I was in the mood for something sweet and romantic to take my mind off my own situation.

"These are our best sellers—I'm sure you'll find something in this pile," the friendly lady said as she pointed me towards the romance section of the store.

I grinned, feeling some of the heaviness in my heart lift as I perused the stack of books. Just what I needed. Since I was an avid reader, I'd need a few to help me through the next few days. I loved getting lost in a novel, taking me to other places and living through the heroine. I just hoped none of them had a life as fucked up as mine. I definitely needed a happily ever after, even if it was only in a novel.

At least I'd always have my dream. It felt so real, the way Oliver had made love to me for the first and only time. The one night that Oliver King belonged to me and said he loved me. I'd always have that; no one could take it away. And because it was a dream, not even Oliver could deny me it. Whenever I needed him, all I had to do was close my eyes and slip back into that dream.

I could relive it a million times—it was mine to keep forever.

Chapter 39
OLIVER

My lungs burned. My head pounded.

I was alone. *So fucking alone.* Abandoned.

But it was so much better than the alternative.

Sinking to the bathroom floor, I let out a long, shuddering breath. At least she didn't do what I feared most. If I absolutely had no choice—if I couldn't have Maya in my life—I'd be gutted. But I'd rather have her alive, knowing that somewhere she was breathing.

Even if it meant I never saw her again, I'd let her go if it meant she kept breathing.

Leaning back against the bathtub, I closed my eyes for a moment.

She always had been free, only she didn't know it. She was the one in control. Always had been. She held my heart in her hands with the power to crush it in one second.

I need to tell her. Find her and tell her.

Reaching for my phone in my pocket, I found the box I'd picked up earlier. Now was as good a time as any to open it. With trembling fingers I pulled the ribbon and took off the lid. I carefully unfolded the yellowed paper. The ink had started to fade and I narrowed my eyes to zone in on the cursive handwriting.

> *These rings represent the circle of life and love.*
> *Your heart will know who the right person is to give it to.*
> *If you are lucky enough to find the ONE, hold on to that love.*
> *Choose wisely.*

Fuck.

Fuck. Fuck. Fuck.

Of course I knew who the rings belonged to. Was my grandmother trying send me a message from the grave? Fuck. Was *Larissa*?

I had to fight for her. Man up and grow the balls to tell her the fucking God's honest truth.

There was no other way.

I'd find her even if it took every day of the rest of my life. I mean, how far could a little bee run from its hive?

I was desperate to find Maya. I closed my eyes for a moment to gather my thoughts. When I opened them a few moments later, my gaze fell on the rubbish bin. She'd left something behind.

Rising to my feet, I peeked into the bin. Blades. Shiny. Unused. She'd thrown them away. Hell, I wasn't a psych expert, but I instinctively knew it was significant. It meant she'd let go of the need to harm herself.

Relief flooded my system. Where would little bee go after taking such a gigantic step? The airport. She'd want to get away from this place, leave her hurt behind. To start fresh—without me.

Exactly where she'd go, I had no clue. The first step was to get to the airport as fast as I could. She couldn't be more than thirty minutes ahead of me. If there was ever a time in my life I needed luck, fate, providence—whatever the hell you wanted to call it—on my side, it was at this moment.

Pressing the button for the escalator, I tapped my foot impatiently, praying that I'd find her. As soon as the doors opened on ground floor, I stepped out and pushed through the revolving doors into the icy cold night. I still had her coat over my arm. She needed it to be warm.

"Airport," I barked at the taxi driver. "Double the fare if you make it in record time."

The man took my challenge, nearly killing us as he sped through the traffic on the icy roads. I didn't care if I died in a car accident. If I didn't find Maya in time, I might as well be dead anyway. Looking back over the last three years, I realized I'd simply existed; I hadn't really lived. I was going to settle for a mediocre life. What a damn fool I was.

I made good on my promise and paid the taxi driver double the fare. I grabbed Maya's coat and ran into the departures building.

Which way?

"All passengers boarding the flight to London, you may proceed to gate eleven."

London.

Sometimes when we'd finished fucking, we'd lie in bed beside each other and talk. She'd tell me little things about her mother. I'd tell her everything I remembered about my father. We kept them alive through our words.

Maya's mother was born in London. She'd told me she always wanted to go there.

I needed a damn ticket to get past security. The line at every ticket counter was miles long, except for one. I was going to need that infamous charm of mine again. More so because the person behind the desk wasn't a woman.

"Good evening, sir," I greeted, trying to sound calm when all I really wanted to do was scream like a crazy person that I needed to get through the gate as soon as possible.

"Yeah?" he said, "How can I help you?"

I took a deep breath. "I need to get to gate eleven. My fiancé is leaving for London. We had a . . . misunderstanding I need to clear up before she goes." His eyes remained glazed over and impersonal. I bet he'd heard all the stories in the book over the years.

I swallowed hard.

Time to get real.

"Look, the truth is, I've fucked up. Badly. She isn't even my fiancé, and she wants nothing to do with me. She hates my guts. But I've just realized I love her. Like, really love her, and I can't let her get on that plane without her knowing."

I exhaled a long breath and waited. Seconds ticked by and still he didn't respond.

"Ahhh, why didn't you just tell me you were an asshole that needed help?" His eyes brightened as a smile twisted his lips.

"Yes, I'm the biggest asshole you ever met in your life. Can you help me?" I was clutching at straws here. The clock was ticking and I was no closer to a resolution.

"Only if you have a valid ticket to fly somewhere, sir."

"What?"

"I said—"

"I heard you. How do I get a ticket?" Shit. I didn't have time for this.

"You're in luck. I was just shutting down for the night, but I like saving assholes from themselves. Happens to be that I was one too, a long time ago."

"Um . . . that's great. So what do I need to do?"

Five minutes later, I had a valid one way ticket in my sweaty hand. Now for security. Luckily I didn't have baggage with me. Taking a hell of a chance, I went to the first class passenger line. It was always shorter.

"I'm running late," I said, shrugging. I nearly kissed the man when he waved me through.

Running as fast as I could, I made my way to gate eleven. She has to be there. As I approached, I started looking for her, frantic that she would be one of the first people to have boarded the plane.

My shoulders dropped as I searched the crowd. Maya was nowhere to be seen. Either she had already boarded or I was mistaken in thinking she was going to London.

I'd come this far, I wasn't giving up without trying everything possible.

I approached the woman at the desk, smiling even though it was the last thing I felt like doing. "Excuse me. I'm wondering if someone I'm looking for has boarded this flight. Can you help me?"

"I'm sorry, sir, I'm not at liberty to give out information on passengers."

"I just want to know if she's on this flight or not."

"What's her name?"

"Maya. Maya Christina Childs."

The woman smiled apologetically. "I'm sorry sir, I don't see that name on my list. That's all I can tell you."

"You know my middle name?" Maya's voice came from behind me.

I spun around, my heart leaping out of my fucking chest.

"Little bee."

"Hello, Oliver," she said, smiling shyly.

"You didn't leave."

"Um, no. Clearly not." She teased me with her eyes. "You didn't need to come all the way to the airport just to bring my coat."

I looked down to where it still hung over my arm. Grinning like a fool, I said, "Thought you'd need it in London. It's freezing there."

She tilted her head and appraised me. "Why did you think I'd go to London of all places?"

"Because of your mother," I answered simply.

She sucked in a breath. "You were listening. All those times I thought I was boring you and you'd gone to sleep because you were so quiet."

"I was listening."

An awkward silence fell between us. She reached out and took her coat from me. My arm felt cold and way too light.

"Thanks for bringing my coat. I was going to buy a new one in London."

"So you were going there!"

"Yes. I was too late to get on that flight—the baggage section had already closed. My flight boards in fifteen minutes."

"Can we talk?"

"What about, Oliver? What's left to say?"

I swallowed hard. "There's too much to talk about here. Come back to my place tonight. We can talk and iron everything out. Then, if you still want to leave, I'll bring you back in the morning and pay for a new ticket. Deal?"

Maya hesitated, dropping her gaze to her hands like she always did.

"Look at me, little bee," I said softly.

Slowly, she raised her head until our eyes met.

My mind flitted back to that night at the pool. The night I'd first realized I loved her.

Really *loved* her.

When I found her there, sleeping on the deck, all I could do at first was stare at her beauty. I saw her vulnerability. The love and peace on her face as I made love to her while she thought she was dreaming. The words I'd held back for years slipped out, spoken to her in her sleep. I knew she heard me. Even if it were a dream, she felt the same. Of that I was sure, even though she'd never spoken of it again.

My chest tightened. I wanted to tell her again. Only this time, I wanted her to be awake and to know it was true. That it wasn't a dream and that I wasn't going to disappear.

If she'd have me, I was hers.

"That dream you had at the pool all those years ago—it wasn't a dream, Maya. It's all true. I love you. Always have. Deep down you knew."

Her eyes shone with tears. "Yes."

"We need to talk. I won't touch you, I promise."

She placed her hand in mine. "Okay, let's go." She smiled up at me, her eyes glowing. "But first we need to get my baggage."

Chapter 40
OLIVER

Maya sobbed into my neck, her tears warm on my skin. "Oh Oliver, I love you so much, but it can never work between us." The sorrow in her voice was undeniable. "We're doomed."

Back in the warmth of my apartment, I'd made us each a hot drink and we'd sat on the sofa, talking for ages about everything we'd been through. At least she admitted that she loved me too. But other than that, it wasn't going my way. Not by a long shot.

Her words pierced my fucking heart. "Don't say that." Closing my eyes to block the sting, I leaned down to press my forehead to hers. "Don't be so afraid, Maya. Follow your instincts—they're always right. Let yourself feel the love in your heart. Don't deny it, please."

Fuck, I had to make her understand. I'd thought about this for far too long, suppressing how I truly felt. Stopped myself from having what I really wanted. That was ending now. No fucking more.

I would kill for her. Maim for her. Go to the depths of hell for her.

And she needed to know.

Of everything I'd done in my life, the one thing I could never regret was falling for Maya and taking her virginity. What I did regret was how I'd handled it.

Even if it angered me at the time that she hadn't told me, I was glad it was me—that I got to be the first. I also planned to be the last. Maya didn't know that yet. I didn't want to scare the bejesus out of my little bee—I'd hardly wrapped my own fucking head around it all.

"This is forbidden. Wrong. *Isn't it?*" Her words were spoken softly, hardly above a whisper. My heart broke for her, feeling her pain as if it were my own. In truth, it was my pain. I needed to take it away.

"Nothing is perfect, my little bee. But no, it can't be wrong to love someone the way I love you."

She sucked in a breath and stared into my eyes, beyond the outer and deep into my fucking soul. I let her gaze, let her see what she wanted to. It was all there—I had nothing to hide. Nothing to be ashamed of.

"Let me show you how it can work. How we're meant to be." I would do anything to make her smile at me again. To make her happy. *Anything*. "I can show you how we're perfect together. Why it's worth it."

"You really believe that?" she said, her body trembling against mine.

I lifted her chin so I could see her face.

"I've loved you forever, Maya. Been intoxicated by you. Thoughts of you consume my mind, sweep me off my feet. My heart has been bleeding all this time we've been apart."

Brushing my lips over hers, her body shuddered before relaxing against mine. She let out a deep sigh.

"So has mine. I'm sorry you've been hurting. I wish I could erase it all."

I believed her.

Pushing her hair off her face and tucking it behind her ear, I cupped my hand around her neck. "I never want to feel that deep ache inside again. Being without you nearly killed me; I was a fool not to do something about it. I thought if I stayed away, I could fix it. Turns out the only thing that was wrong was me."

She reached out a hand to stroke my cheek. Her eyes sparkled. "We did what we thought we had to do."

My lips twisted into a melancholic smile. "I thought what I did would be best for you, even if it killed me inside."

She smiled. "Silly boy."

Gazing into her eyes, I wanted to know the truth. "Little bee, what do you really want? What is your deepest heart's desire?" I let out a long shuddering breath, hoping she'd say what I wanted to hear.

She didn't hesitate. "I want to be everything to you," she whispered.

"You mean that?"

"Uh-huh," she hummed. It was the sweetest sound. "I want to be all you ever need."

"You are, baby. You're that and so much more. My need for you is all-consuming, never ending. It has no beginning or end it just is."

She blinked a few times, tears still shimmering on her lashes. "That's the sweetest thing you've ever said."

"I love you so fucking much it hurts." My voice was raw.

Love radiated through my being, bursting through every cell in my body. I couldn't hide it if I tried. The tears that were brimming in her beautiful eyes splashed onto her cheeks. I sucked them up, one by one, drinking her in.

"All those years . . . I wish I knew," she said, sorrow returning to her eyes.

"You did. We both did. But society made it hard on us. I tried to conform, tried to be reasonable. It's just bullshit—I can't do it any more. When a love like this comes along . . . only a fool would deny it." I grinned. "I'm an idiot, but I ain't no fool, baby."

She chuckled softly, her body reverberating against mine, sending delicious tingles up the length of my spine.

"Something's been missing for the longest time," I sighed into her hair.

"What?"

"Just being inside you. I'm sorry for the time I wasted when we could've been happy. Could've been making love."

Her smile shone through her tears and nearly made my heart stop. "It was never wasted; it just made us grow stronger. Love one another more."

"Yes, it did. We will make time stop just for us. So we can catch up. Because I can never get enough of you."

Maya laughed as I pulled her closer. "Enough talking. Time to catch up, baby."

I swept her up in my arms and carried her to the bed, lying her down gently. I wasn't going to be able to take it slow the first time. "First I'm going to fuck you. Hard. Then I'm going to make love to you," I said as I stripped off my clothes. I couldn't wait to get inside her.

This time I would really make her mine. This time Maya was willingly giving herself to me.

No threats or bribes. No monster tactics. No hidden agendas.

Nothing between us but love and a need to be united in every possible way.

A man and his woman. Simple. Profound. Beautiful.

With a gruff voice, I made a promise. "I'm going to make time stop for us."

Chapter 41
MAYA

ONE YEAR ON

Oliver stroked my growing belly.

"So you're sure it's a girl?" he asked.

I laughed at the expression on his face. "Yep, in the absence of a penis, it's usually a girl. So pink it is. You win."

Since I'd found out that I was pregnant sixteen weeks ago, we'd been at odds about the sex of the baby. I wanted a little boy—just like Oliver. He wanted a girl from the start. As always, he got his way.

"I still can't believe it. We're naming her Hope like we agreed? And her second name after your mother?" His eyes were trained on me as he waited for affirmation.

I nodded. I didn't really mind that it wasn't a boy; she was only the first of a whole team. Oliver and I decided on the day we got married, nearly twelve months ago now in London, that we never wanted to have an only child. We wanted our babies to belong to a family of brothers and sisters—with two loving parents who couldn't get enough of one another.

Lying back against the pillows of our king size bed, I studied his handsome face. His hair was tousled from messing around earlier and I could swear his stubble had grown in the last hour. I wanted his face back between my thighs, his stubble brushing against my skin.

Oliver slipped his hands over my bare skin and squeezed my boobs gently, then weighed them both in his hands.

"Fuck, little bee, these tits are getting bigger by the week. I can't keep my hands off you."

"Not that I want you to—being pregnant is making me so fucking horny all the time. It's all your damn fault," I said, laughing as I poked him playfully in the chest.

"Baby, you know what poking me like that does to me," he warned.

I poked harder. "What? Tell me."

"It makes me want to ravish your body. Eat your pussy. *Fuck you*," he growled.

"Always so good with words, Mr. King."

"Always such a tease, Mrs. King. You make me want you all the fucking time."

"Good. That *is* my intention, in case you haven't noticed."

He grinned and stared down at my breasts as if he'd never seen them before.

"My eyes are up here, baby," I teased.

"I know, but right this minute I wanna check out my tits. See how they've grown. Suck them, lick them. Then later, when I'm buried deep inside you, that's when I'll give your eyes my attention."

His words made my pussy clench. Making love with Oliver was my favorite thing to do. He took care of my every need. But the very best part was near the end, when his fingers laced with mine, him rocking his hard cock inside me while staring into the depths of my soul. It never got old.

"I've always known you were the only one for me—I was just too stubborn to admit it." He kissed me hard, bruising my lips under his. Eventually letting go, he pulled back so he could see my face, wiping his thumb over my lips. "I lusted after these bee-stung lips. To taste your breath."

He moved down my body and sucked a nipple into his mouth. "Since these tits were nothing but bee stings they've driven my cock crazy."

"Oh yeah?" I murmured, willing him to go further.

His hand—the one wearing a platinum wedding ring—smoothed softly over my belly, traveling south. A soft chuckle rose from his chest as my knees fell open of their own accord, offering him my very core, eager for his touch. His fingers traced the lips of my pussy, causing my whole body to quiver in anticipation.

"God, you turn me into your slut every time you do that. I can't keep my legs together when you touch me like that," I moaned.

"Mmmm, I dreamed of this pussy ever since the first time you tortured me by pressing up against the window naked. Do you have any idea how that fucked with my head?"

"Yeah, you've told me . . . but tell me again," I said, basking in the delight of his thumb slowly circling my clit.

"I could smell your arousal every time you were near me. Your singular scent turned my cock the fuck on so hard I couldn't handle it sometimes. I tried to stop it from taking over, but I never could. Trying to ignore you—ignore this pussy—was one of the biggest challenges of my life."

"Until you couldn't anymore," I said, already knowing where this story was going.

"When I found you bleeding on the tile, it was as if my heart was ripped out of my fucking body. Losing you—just the thought was enough to make me fucking crazy. That's when I decided I had to have you at all costs. Only I knew you wouldn't do it."

"So you blackmailed me. Not knowing that it was exactly what I wanted. I was your slut, and even though I didn't know it at the time, it was what I was born to do. Belong to you."

His eyes softened. "Baby, you have no fucking idea what those words mean to me. That you're giving yourself to me because you want to."

"I've always wanted you. Everything I ever did was to make you see me. To taunt you into fucking me."

"You did a damn fine job of that. My dick just wouldn't listen to my brain. I was supposed to be older, smarter. But you won. I couldn't resist you."

His thumb pressed harder on my nub, then slipped between my wet and swollen folds. Talking was becoming near impossible.

"My beautiful little bee. Nothing beats the first time I tasted you on my tongue. Sweet like honey." His head dipped between my legs and out of sight behind the bump between us. My back arched off the bed as he took one long sweep over my pussy. Oliver's trademark, he called it. I would kill for it. "You still are. Sweet," he mumbled with his mouth on my pussy.

I lifted my ass off the bed, offering him more of me, biting into my bottom lip as he ate me out. I whimpered like a wanton slut as two fingers moved inside me.

"Oliver, fuck me," I begged, wanting his cock inside me.

"I love it when you beg. Almost as much as I love when you say my name in that husky voice."

"Oliver, *please*," I begged again. "Stop talking and fuck me."

He flipped me onto my side and lay behind me, slipping his cock into me slowly while his thumb kept circling my clit. No way was I going to last.

Oliver's breath was warm on my skin. "This is what I live and breathe for, Maya. Being inside you."

Those words were all I needed to spiral into a mind blowing orgasm. I gasped for air as his pace picked up, his cock slamming into me from behind.

"I need to see your eyes," he grunted. I twisted my body and threw a leg over his, making the penetration of his cock so much deeper. Turning my face to his, our eyes locked.

"Perfect. You are fucking perfect, Mrs. King."

"So are you. For me."

"I fucking love you," he roared, his cock exploding inside me.

"I know," I whispered. "I love you, too. Make time stand still, Oliver."

He did. His mouth stole mine, and nothing existed but us.

"You've tamed the monster, little bee. All I want is you. Nothing else."

I snuggled into him, pushing my ass back so he stayed inside me. I was completely exhausted. "Sleep now, love." His warm breath caressed over the shell of my ear and I let my whole body go limp in his strong embrace.

I drifted off to sleep. One hand on my belly, the other on my pussy, and Oliver's cock deep inside me. Just the way it was meant to be. I loved it.

Epilogue

I looked down at the curly dark head of my baby girl and smiled. Six-week-old Hope Megan King was the most precious thing in my life. Besides her father, of course.

Oliver had become twitchy after she was born, working from his office in our London apartment so he could constantly check on me and our baby.

I'd never been as happy as this in my entire life, but he was concerned that I'd follow in my mother's footsteps. And that's why we ended up staying in London. He helped me track down her family—my family—so I could get to know the woman she was before she moved away to marry my father.

Larissa and Daddy were devoted grandparents, but they understood why we didn't want to live in California. They visited us pretty frequently and the spare room was always ready for them.

We stood in the baby's room, listening to her breathe. Oliver had pulled me into his embrace, our foreheads touching, yet I could feel tension in the air.

"Stop worrying about me, baby," I chided softly. "I'm never leaving you, or our baby girl."

He pulled away just enough so he could stare down at me.

"Fuck, Maya, if you ever left me—I can't even imagine what your father went through losing Megan."

"I know. It was tough on him. He missed her so much."

"At least he always had you."

"And he's happy now with Larissa. She's really good for him."

"I'm glad you—we—are getting on better with her now. She seems a lot more content in her own skin." He chuckled at his own lame joke.

"If it weren't for Larissa, and her obsession with plastic surgery, we would never have met. Ever thought of that?"

"Sure have, baby. Who would have helped me overcome my demons and healed my damaged soul if it weren't for you?"

"How did you know I was the one and not Bianca?" I still couldn't say her name without unease bubbling up in my stomach. Although she'd moved on and married some Danish billionaire with one foot in the grave, I'd never like that woman. It was just the way it was.

"My grandmother's rings. The note she wrote. When I read what she'd written, I knew the real answer. I could deny it all I wanted, but you were the only one for me."

"And you for me," I said as I lifted my mouth to his for a kiss.

"I love you, little bee."

"I love you, Oliver. With all my heart, body and soul. I am yours—every part of me."

He sighed against my ear. "Those are the sweetest words I've ever heard."

He swooped me into his arms. "My cock wants you again. Let's get some practice making Hope's little brother while she's off in dreamland."

I slapped him against his chest. "Holy shit, don't you ever get tired of fucking?"

"With you—never. But tonight I want to make love to you. Slow and easy."

"Like in my dreams?" I whispered.

"Like in your dreams."

"Make time stand still, Oliver."

He did.

The End

ACKNOWLEDGEMENTS

It takes a village to publish a book and I'd be lost without my village.

Firstly, I need to thank my beautiful family for putting up with me while I wrote this book. A lot of hours went into it and you guys gave me those hours. I owe you. And I love you. Thank you.

To my beta readers and editor, Dawn, I could not have done this book without you all! You read over my work time and time again and listened to me on the phone at all hours while we discussed Oliver and Maya. Thank you for encouraging me to keep going, especially in those hours where I felt like it was all a big mess.

To my lovely cover designer, LJ from Mayhem Cover Creations, thank you so much for your gorgeous cover! And for putting up with my many changes. You are so fast and reliable and I will sing your praises everywhere I go.

To Kylie from Give Me Books. Thank you so much for taking me on at the last minute and guiding me. Also, thank you for putting up with me when life got a bit hectic and things didn't go as planned. I am very thankful to have found you.

To the amazing bloggers who helped me promote this book. Wow! The response I received from you all has been nothing short of amazing and I am so thankful for all the help you have given me.

To my readers. Thank you for reading Monster Stepbrother. Thank you for your excitement about this book! I hope you love Oliver and Maya as much as I do.

FEARLESS FIGHTER

Are you ready for Quinn's Story?

Coming Soon!

Pain is all I've ever known.

Mental. Emotional. Physical.

Ingrained into my soul, I can't live without it. Pain is who I am. Pain is what makes me breathe.

The need to inflict it on others consumes me.

I need it to ease my demons. To get through my days. To get off.

I meticulously plan my life around my depravity. The innocent must be protected. I lost control once, and I refuse to allow it to happen again.

Fighting is my savior, as are the women who crave the pain as much as I do.

Through fighting and women I keep my darkest urges under control.

And then Quinn comes back into my life.

The one woman I've always craved.

The one woman who doesn't want the pain.

The one woman I've fought so hard to walk away from.

She awakens the beast inside me, and I'm not sure I can control myself any more.

I'm not sure I want to.

*****

CONTACT DETAILS

I love hearing from readers.
You can find me here:

Facebook
https://www.facebook.com/authorharlowgrace

Twitter
@harlowgauthor

Email
authorharlowgrace@gmail.com